What the Duke Wants

by

Kristin Vayden

What the Duke Wants
by Kristin Vayden
Published by Blue Tulip Publishing
www.bluetulippublishing.com

This is a work of fiction. Names, places, characters, and events are fictitious in every regard. Any similarities to actual events and persons, living or dead, are purely coincidental. Any trademarks, service marks, product names, or named features are assumed to be the property of their respective owners, and are used only for reference. There is no implied endorsement if any of these terms are used. Except for review purposes, the reproduction of this book in whole or part, electronically or mechanically, constitutes a copyright violation.

WHAT THE DUKE WANTS
Copyright © 2014 KRISTIN VAYDEN
ISBN 13: 978-1499308402
ISBN: 149930840X
Cover Art Designed by P.S. Cover Design

Chapter One

Charles Evermore, Duke of Clairmont, glared at his solicitor, narrowing his eyes until he could no longer see the small framed man before him. There had to be a mistake. There was no other explanation for the words coming from the man's mouth.

"Your grace, if you'll simply read the documentation for yourself..." Mr. Burrows spoke with practiced patience.

Charles stood and stalked around the desk, ripping the papers from his grasp. Mr. Burrows leaned back, folding his hands and watching Charles with unaffected impassivity. Not for the first time, Charles thought the man looked like a praying mantis, all long and lean with exceedingly large eyes and a patient demeanor that was all to deceptive.

But he was the best solicitor available.

He had better be for what Charles paid for his services.

"If you'll start on the second page..." Mr. Burrows suggested.

Charles read the endless prattle of legal terms until his eyes focused on the chilling phrase.

Wards.

Three girls, to be exact. Ranging from ages seven to sixteen.

And, as heaven stood by laughing, he was to be their guardian.

Charles stared at the words, willing them to disappear. He hadn't the time, the energy, or the inclination to take over the raising of three insufferable miniature females! He could hardly tolerate his mistresses, and they were full grown and low maintenance! He studied the rest of the document, searching for any other names that might take this plight away from him.

"You're likely curious as to why you were chosen," Mr. Burrows suggested.

"The question had crossed my mind." Charles remarked sarcastically.

Mr. Burrows wisely ignored the duke's surly attitude. "It was a tragedy, to be sure. The poor girls lost both parents in a carriage accident—"

"And there were no aunts or uncle to take them in?" Charles interrupted.

Mr. Burrows simply blinked, raising his eyebrows slightly and waiting.

"Carry on." Charles waved his hand, somewhat chagrined at his idiotic question. After all, if there *were* a spinster aunt or bachelor uncle, hell, any relative at all, they wouldn't be given to him as wards.

"As I was saying…" Mr. Burrows shot Charles a pointed gaze. "The girls were left quite without any family. Only providence connected them with you, your grace. You see, they are actually your mother's second cousins, God rest her soul."

"So I'm the urchins' cousin? Bloody perfect." Charles mumbled under his breath.

"So it would seem." Mr. Burrows stood, collecting the papers from Charles's outstretched hand. "You'll not need to worry about a dowry or any such things for the young ladies. Their parents left them quite a bit of wealth. However, I would suggest you begin a search for a proper governess."

"Bloody hell, another female in my house. Exactly what I need."

"Yes, well, that female might be your salvation in helping you train the children into young ladies. After all, they'll need to someday make a match."

"That's the only way I'm ever going to be rid of them, isn't it?" Charles combed back his jet-black hair with his hand, feeling a miserable headache beginning at the base of his neck.

"Perhaps." Mr. Burrows nodded and turned away, but not before Charles saw the slightest hint of a grin. "The young ladies will arrive in a few days, I expect. If you need anything more, you know where to reach me. Good night, your grace." Mr. Burrows paused at the door.

"Good night, Mr. Burrows."

Charles strode over to the fire, studying the orange and red flames. Truly, this was the worst sort of news. At three and thirty, he wasn't necessarily old, but he was quite accustomed and comfortable with his way of life. Oh, he knew eventually he'd have to suffer through a woman's presence enough to marry her and produce an heir, but he still figured he had at least five years before that would be necessary.

And to be sure, he was waiting until it was absolutely necessary.

A few days, a mere forty-eight hours and his entire existence would be in upheaval. To think, only four hours ago he was looking forward to a cozy evening with Céline, the opera diva he had sequestered in a little townhouse not far away. Under the present circumstances, he no longer was looking forward to anything. Rather, he was quite content to stand before the fire and feel sorry for himself.

Of course! He could take the girls to the country and leave them there with a governess.

Why hadn't he thought of it before? It was a stroke of brilliance. He needn't have his life interrupted after all! Surely the young ladies wouldn't want him around anyhow. Why, he'd only be in the way. A governess would be infinity more suitable for them. He needn't interfere!

Suddenly the evening was brighter, even the fire cast a cheerier glow about the room. All he had to do was secure a governess. And that couldn't be hard to do. He'd simply inquire about and interview prospective persons. Better yet, Mrs. Pott, the housekeeper, could interview. She'd be far more capable and wise in knowing what made a good governess.

Charles congratulated himself on his brilliant plan and to celebrate, strode over to the liquor cabinet, and poured himself a glass of amber-colored brandy.

"Cheers," he murmured.

Already those girls were as good as gone.

****

Two Days Later, Near Bath.

Mr. Burrows regarded his young client, impressed with the poise and grace in one so young. Why, she couldn't be a day over eighteen. Miss Carlotta Standhope was uncommonly pretty, it was a shame that she'd not have a come out. The *ton* would have celebrated her golden hair and clear green eyes, but it was her character that made her supremely appealing, he decided.

It must have been a severe blow for her to discover the future she'd anticipated was no longer available to her. It was part of his business, delivery of unwelcome news. However the young woman was taking it all in with such grace and poise, it caused him to greatly respect the young woman. Pity pinched his heart. Unaccustomed to any emotional response when dealing with his clients, he fidgeted with his spectacles

"I'm sure you'd like a moment..." He stood to leave, offering her a moment to gather herself in private.

"No, please." Her green eyes widened as she visibly swallowed. "I need to understand the full depth of my change in situation. Please...continue." She took a deep breath as if fortifying herself.

"Very well, Miss Standhope." He nodded then resumed his seat. "As I know you're aware, upon you parents passing several years ago, the substantial inheritance they left for you was primarily invested overseas, in the Caribbean. The interest from that investment has been what you've lived on these past years. I'm sorry to say that with the recent tropical cyclone, the investment in the Caribbean was a total loss."

"Total, as in I'm penniless, or total as in I'll still have enough food to eat and won't be turned out of my own home?" she asked her voice cracking.

"Garden Gate is entailed, so you'll not lose the manor or lands, but you'll also not have any funds to maintain their upkeep."

"So, it's as good as being completely penniless."

"Yes, I'm afraid so."

"I see." Her slight shoulders slumped as if carrying a burden to heavy to bear.

"However, you could possibly lease the land and manor out, not requiring you to sell. That could produce some revenue."

"That could work. But what, then, of me? What am I to do?" Tears welled, glistening in her eyes and, though none fell, her green orbs took on the luminosity of glowing emeralds. Captivated by her venerable gaze, Mr. Burrows struggled to find some good news to give the poor young woman.

"I'm not sure, Miss Standhope. Do you have relatives you can impose upon?"

"None that I'm aware of."

He leaned back against the chair and a thought tickled his

mind. Studying her one more, he nodded. Perhaps he did have some promising news to offer after all.

"I see. Are you…are you perhaps willing to consider employment?"

****

Carlotta stiffened at the idea of employment. Her father hadn't been a high-ranking earl or marquis, but even as a baron, he had impressed upon his daughter the place and position of the titled. It chafed to think of working, of becoming a bluestocking, but she saw no other options available.

She was rather fond of having food to eat and didn't plan on starving to death.

"I'm willing—" Carlotta swallowed and drew a breath to compose herself. "I'm willing to seek employment." She folded her hands in her lap, clutching them tightly.

"A governess or companion position would be quite suitable, I'd imagine."

"Governess, yes. I could do quite well in that position. I'm well educated, you know." Carlotta's mind began to spin with possibilities. Being a governess wouldn't be half bad. She could do it, she was certain.

She could hear her own heartbeat, its pounding cadence reminded her that she was, indeed, alive when she felt like she had shriveled up and died. To think, only hours before she had been planning her wardrobe for the season and daydreaming about her first kiss.

None of it was to be. None. In the span of ten minutes, her entire world had come crashing down upon her, leaving nothing but rubble.

"If you don't mind," said Mr. Burrows as he took off his spectacles and leaned forward slightly, his balding head shining, "I have a client who might be interested in hiring you.

If you wish, I'll make arrangements for an interview."

Could she do it? Work? Leave behind all she knew? Carlotta glanced about the parlor, studying the tall windows that overlooked the small gardens. It wasn't grand, but it was home. And if she took a position as governess, she'd be leaving it all behind to a stranger. But what choice did she have?

"Thank you, Mr. Burrows. I'd appreciate the opportunity."

****

Charles Evermore, Duke of Clairmont

Carlotta studied the card and swallowed a lump of fear that lodged itself in her throat. Of course, she would be interviewing for a position in the devil's lair. That was precisely the kind of luck she was having recently. Not only had her trunks fallen off the carriage on her way to London, resulting in all of her clothes being muddied and some torn, but also, she had caught a chill. Thank heavens she'd been able to secure some elderberry tea. But regardless, the resulting sniffle wasn't proper governess behavior at all. It would be a miracle for her to get this position, but as she studied the name on the card sent from Mr. Burrows, she wondered if maybe God was protecting her. Surely, there were other positions that didn't involve bargaining the devil.

It was well known among the *ton* and those who gossiped about them, that the Duke of Clairmont was not the type of man to cross. Although deliciously handsome —at least that's what the rumor said— he had a reputation that boasted his arrogant nature and intolerance for women beyond their company in his bedroom —or their bedroom, for that matter. Carlotta's cheeks heated with a blush at simply thinking those words. True, he could have his pick of any of the season's Incomparables, but he wasn't marriage minded.

At least not yet. His hair was as dark as sin with eyes that were the color of a summer sky. His tall and powerful frame exuded power and dominance, shrinking down all other men in the room. Of course, one could not always believe the gossip.

Especially when it said he had kept no fewer than a dozen mistresses at one time. Certainly, *that* was exaggerated. Nevertheless, the stories about the handsome duke abounded and grew to mammoth proportions. Which was why Carlotta had to summon all her courage to walk up the steps to his home.

The one question that remained quite a mystery was why the duke needed a governess at all. It was well known he was a confirmed bachelor. Could he have a brood of children born on the wrong side of the blanket? Carlotta highly doubted it. After all, based on the gossip, he didn't seem like the doting father type. No, with his reputation, he'd toss the poor woman unfortunate enough to have gotten pregnant, into the streets. Yes, his soul was a black as his hair. Of course, having never seen the duke in person, Carlotta could only imagine how dark his hair really was.

She walked to the door and knocked, willing her racing heartbeat to slow its galloping pulse.

"Yes?" an aged butler inquired.

"Miss Carlotta Standhope. I'm here to interview for the governess position. I'm here on Mr. Burrows' recommendation," she spoke her practiced words.

"Yes. Wait a moment." The butler left her on the doorstep but returned less than a minute later.

"Mrs. Pott will be conducting your interview in the parlor. If you'll follow me."

Carlotta tried not to appear too curious as she studied the bachelor lodgings of one of the most notorious rakes of the *ton*. Dark woods covered the walls and rich rugs softened the floors. It was pristine and clean yet dark and brooding all at once. As she glanced about, she decided it had to be from the lack of light. For it being daylight outside, it was quite dark inside.

The butler opened a door that was already slightly ajar and waited for Carlotta to enter. As she did, a plump woman no younger than sixty years greeted her. She was cheery, her cheeks rosy and her smile warm. Carlotta felt a bit more at ease.

"I'm pleased to meet you, Miss Standhope. You come on excellent recommendation," the woman greeted warmly.

"Thank you."

"Where are my manners? Forgive me, darling. I'm Mrs. Pott, his grace's housekeeper. You'll have to excuse me. I'm not accustomed to interviewing governesses. Please, come and sit. Let's have us a chat, shall we?" She gestured to a chair opposite her and Carlotta sat.

"Murray? Would you please have tea brought up?"

The butler nodded and disappeared.

"Now then, why don't we begin with you telling a bit about yourself, Miss Standhope."

"I'm nineteen this year, Mrs. Pott, and well versed in Latin, French as well as classic literature, mathematics and some of the more popular sciences. I studied under my own tutor until recent circumstances required me to seek my own employment." Carlotta held her breath, hoping the words she'd rehearsed were neither too rushed nor divulged too much information on her current straits.

"I see. You're quite the educated woman it seems." Mrs. Pott nodded.

"Thank you."

"Now then, have you experience in how to conduct oneself in social situations? The duke has become the guardian of three young women, all in need of guidance not only in their formal education but in other social graces."

"Yes, I'm able to guide them in the various social situations they'll likely encounter being associated with his grace," Carlotta responded confidently.

"Lovely. His grace plans on moving the girls to his country estate in Bath. Do you have any connections that would prohibit your moving from London?"

"No." Yet her heart pinched. Bath was awfully close to Garden Gate. What miserable torture to be so near one's home yet so completely away at the same time!

"Delightful. Then, Miss Standhope, I'm extending the offer of employment to you, should you wish to accept. You seem very well suited for the position and with such a glowing recommendation, I'd be daft to not welcome you to his grace's staff."

"Thank you, Mrs. Pott. I humbly accept." Carlotta barely resisted the urge to let out a huge sigh of relief. That had certainly been much easier than she had anticipated.

"Now then, that's settled. We'll have us a spot of tea and then I'll take you to meet your charges. They are currently staying here, but will be traveling shortly. I'm assuming you'll need to quit your current lodgings as well?"

"Yes, it shan't take long."

"No need to worry. I'll have Murray task someone with fetching your belongings and ensuring your account is settled."

"Oh, there's not need, I can—"

"Of course there's a need my dear. You'll find that, being in the duke's employ that, while his reputation is less than above reproach, he is generous and kind to those he employs. I'm quite sure he'd be put out if I did any less for you, my dear."

"Well, thank you." Carlotta tried to be gracious but all she could think of was the sorry state of most of her clothing due to the muddy descent from the carriage. Hopefully, whoever collected her belongings wouldn't look *too* closely.

Chapter Two

Carlotta glanced about her room, still shocked that it had been assigned to someone under employ. The large bed boasted the softest feather mattress and the light blue of the walls gave the room a relaxing atmosphere. How strange, she thought, to feel so at ease in a duke's private residence. She almost laughed out loud, if not for the tiny fear that someone might hear. She walked to the dressing table and sat. In short work, she unbound and re-twisted her hair into a respectable and much tidier knot at the back of her head. A wave of sadness crashed over her at the remembrance that there would be no season for her, no beautiful gowns, no gentlemen asking for dances, no stolen kisses. But at least she wouldn't go hungry, and with any luck, Mr. Burrows would find a tenant for Garden Gate. No, she would be thankful for small blessings, for the small blessings added up into large ones. Indeed, things could be far worse.

A knock on her door brought her head up and she rose. "Yes?"

"It is I, Mrs. Pott, dear. Your belongings just arrived," the housekeeper answered as she let herself into the room.

"Thank you."

"I, er..." Mrs. Pott stuttered, her cheerful face slightly pinched in concern. "I'm afraid some of your clothes were, shall we say, damaged, in some sort."

"Yes, I'm aware. It was why I was hesitant for you to collect them. You see, on my way to London, my trunk fell and opened on impact. My dresses and—other things—didn't manage too well against the mud on the road." Carlotta felt her face flush with humiliation.

"You poor dear! How wretched! I'll have them laundered and pressed at once. Whatever can't be salvaged, I'll endeavor to have new dresses made to replace them."

"There's no need, I'm sure what I have will suffice." The last thing she wanted was to be an imposition.

"Oh fustian! Remember, my dear, your employer is the duke. We cannot have you looking like you work for anyone less."

"Oh, I hadn't thought—"

"Not to worry, dear. You'll get used to it. Now, shall I introduce you to the girls?"

"Yes." Carlotta exhaled a sigh of relief.

"Very well, follow me and I'll take to you them."

Carlotta followed Mrs. Pott's plump figure down the hall and to the left. It was oddly quiet for there being three children about. She expected Mrs. Pott to lead her to another floor, but rather, she paused in front of a large wooden door and knocked softly. Carlotta watched her expression soften. "Girls? I've your new governess with me."

The door cracked open slightly. Two very large brown eyes glanced out warily.

"Yes m'um." The door continued to open.

Mrs. Pott cut a glance to Carlotta, speaking volumes. She would need to tread carefully.

They entered a large salon decorated in a cream color. A cheery fire danced in the hearth, but the tone, the overall feeling of the room was one of despair. Carlotta focused on the two other girls sitting together on the settee, holding hands. The third girl joined them shortly. Clearly older, she placed a protective arm around the other two as she watched their approach with careful consideration.

It was apparent they were all sisters. Three pairs of chocolate colored eyes were all framed in dark feathery eyelashes. Wide lips were thinned in a wary line and their chestnut hair was plaited neatly and in a similar fashion. In all truth, they looked like the very same girl but in different stages of life. The youngest couldn't be older than seven and the middle one looked to be about ten or eleven. The oldest was perhaps fourteen but that was uncertain. She was in the first bloom of a young lady but her eyes seemed older, wiser. Pained.

"Beatrix, Bethanny, Roberta? This is Miss Standhope. She is to be your governess," said Mrs. Pott by way of introduction.

"Berty, my name is Berty," the youngest corrected with a scowl before being hushed by her older sister.

"Yes, well." Mrs. Pott tried to hide a grin.

"Hello, sweet girls. I'm pleased to meet you." Carlotta spoke quietly. Then on impulse, she took a few steps to get closer. Crouching down, she met them at eye level. "Truly, I am pleased to make your acquaintance. You're all entirely lovely and I'm sure we'll get along quite well."

Berty, the youngest, smiled, revealing a missing front tooth. However, the older two simply nodded, their expressions inscrutable.

I'll leave you to get acquainted. Dinner will be shortly." Mrs. Pott left, closing the door behind her.

"Now then, can you please tell me which of you is Beatrix and which one is Bethanny?" Carlotta asked, standing.

"I'm Beatrix," the middle girl stated, her voice was deeper than Carlotta expected, a true mezzo.

"I'm Bethanny," the oldest spoke next, her voice clear and pure.

"I'm Carlotta but you must call me Lottie. It's ever so much easier than Carlotta," she said with a grin.

"I like you," Berty stated.

"Well I like you as well." Carlotta reached out and patted the girl's shoulder tenderly. "So, why don't you tell me a little about yourselves? Bethanny? Would you start please?"

"Well, I'm sixteen. I'm fond of reading and have done quite well with my embroidery."

"How ladylike."

"Thank you. Momma—"

She stopped, her eyes darting to her lap as she bit her lower lip. The two other girls took similar postures.

"Your mother? Was embroidery important to her?" Carlotta went out on a limb, hoping she wasn't hurting their fragile relationship.

"Yes," came a low whisper.

"You know, I lost my parents as well when I was about your age, Bethanny," said Carlotta, keeping her voice gentle.

All three girls gave her their rapt attention, pain and understanding clear on their faces.

"Really?" Beatrix asked.

"Yes, they took ill. My mother died of pneumonia and my father took to his bed shortly after. I think perhaps, he didn't know how to live without my mother. He died about a month after her. "

"That's horrid." This from Berty.

"It was indeed."

"What did you do?" asked Beatrix.

"I wept...a lot. Tears clean your soul, you know. They help wash away the pain. And with time, the pain becomes less and less. You forget how sad you are and remember how happy you were when they were alive."

"I miss Momma and my father too," Berty confided.

"I'm sure you do." Carlotta reached up and smoothed a stray lock of chestnut hair on the child's head. "But you're not truly alone. You have your sisters. And together you can all remember all the lovely things about your parents that made them so special. And as you get older, you can share the most delicious secrets together, and encourage one another."

"I suppose that's true," Bethanny said, a thoughtful expression flitting across her beautiful face.

"It is true."

"Do you have sisters, Miss Lottie?" Beatrix asked.

"No. I always wished I did. So you see how lucky you are?"

"Yes."

"Very good. Now. Tell me about yourself, Beatrix." Carlotta coaxed.

"I'm eleven, and I hate to read. I'd much rather be outside. I love riding but..." She leaned forward as if to impart some great secret.

Carlotta leaned in, an indulgent smile tickling her lips.

"I hate sidesaddle. Father let me ride astride, like a boy!"

"Heavens!" Carlotta feigned shock, her lips spreading into a grin.

"Truly! But he always said as I grew older I'd need to learn sidesaddle." She pouted.

"That's wise."

Beatrix regarded Carlotta with a curious expression. "Do you ride sidesaddle?"

"Yes, I do."

"Then you can teach me." She nodded.

"I'm sure there will be a great many things we'll learn from each other." Carlotta replied. "Now then, little Berty, your full name is Roberta, correct?"

"Yes, but I hate it. Roberta." She said the name in a whine. "All it is, is a boy's name with a 'a' at the end. Honestly, couldn't Mother think of a proper girl's name for me? They said they were glad I was a girl but I think they wanted a boy. You know, to name him Robert. They were stuck with me so they just added a 'a' to the end."

"My." Carlotta blinked, not quite sure how to address such a statement. "I'm sure your parents were thrilled to have another girl. And, I'll have you know, Roberta is quite a popular name for a girl. You're parents didn't just make it up on a whim."

"That's what I keep telling her." Bethanny rolled her eyes.

"I still don't like it. Call me Berty, please."

"Fine, Miss Berty. You know, you even look like a Berty, now that I think of it."

"I always thought so too." The seven-year-old nodded sagely.

"Now then, shall I tell you about myself?" Carlotta asked the girls.

"Yes!" Berty shouted while the other two nodded.

"Well, I'm a bit older than your oldest sister, so I'll have plenty to teach you. I'm versed in Latin, French, and all the other studies you'll need to learn. But also of equal importance, I'll be teaching you how to be ladies of quality. Was your father titled?"

"Yes, he was a baron," Bethanny said.

"So was my father," Carlotta spoke before thinking.

"Then why—" Bethanny's expression was confused.

"It's not important. You are now the wards of a very powerful and influential duke. You'll need to be properly trained in the ways of the London elite."

"Will we go to balls?" This from Beatrix.

"I'm sure you will."

"And drink champagne?" This from Berty.

"When you're much older. So you see, you have so many wonderful things to look forward to."

"I suppose." Bethanny nodded with a thoughtful

expression.

A knock sounded at the door. "Yes?" Carlotta answered.

Murray entered. "Dinner is served."

"Lovely. Thank you." Carlotta stood, her charges mimicking her movements.

"Let's follow Mr. Murray while he escorts us to dinner."

They went down the hall and soon the heavenly fragrance of roasted duck with some sort of rich sauce assaulted Carlotta's senses. It had been an age, it seemed, since she had enjoyed a proper meal. At least since the fretful day Mr. Burrows had come to call. She'd found her appetite had quite disappeared, and then when it returned, she was already on her way to London and the fare she procured wasn't of the tempting variety.

They entered a gilded dining room with gleaming picture frames and polished sconces that reflected the candlelight in a deep glow. Velvet-covered chairs of deep crimson offered soft and luxurious respite as they all sat down to the table. While the room was large enough to accommodate at least fifty, the extra leaves had been removed from the table, which made it much smaller, though still far too large for the small party about to dine.

Dinner was served with a grand flourish, each dish as beautifully displayed as it was delicious. Carlotta kept her eye on the girls, watching their table manners and tucking little observances into the back of her mind for later instruction. A voice boomed in the hall, giving her quite the start.

"I don't care if it's the bloody Noah's flood! They can't be here tomorrow! I'm… entertaining," the dominant male voice shouted, clearly the duke and therefore not accustomed to other people in hearing distance within his own home.

Carlotta heard Murray's voice but was unable to distinguish his words. It was quiet then, too quiet. Carlotta glanced at the girls. They were all staring at their plates, their eating long ceased as they clearly understood the meaning behind the loud shouts.

They weren't wanted.

And nothing could have angered Carlotta more. Right then she decided, regardless of what Mrs. Pott said about the duke caring about his servants, all the gossip concerning him had to be truth. He was arrogant and thought only of himself. Truly, it was maddening for someone with so much power, wealth and influence to be so concerned with just himself. However, she didn't need the girls sharing her opinion, though she rather thought they'd figure it out soon enough. As their guardian, they needed to respect the duke, regardless.

"Girls, in spite of what you heard, remember that the duke is taking very good care of you. You're fed, you have a warm place to sleep, and now you have me. I imagine it is quite a difficult adjustment for him as well. Let us have grace for, well, his grace. Shall we?"

****

Charles wiped his face with his white-gloved hand at the gentle and unaccountably forgiving tone of the woman just on the other side of the door. Thoroughly shamed, not only by his butler, who had calmly reminded him that his guests were nearby and therefore privy to his loud declaration, but now by the lowly governess also. There was only so much humbling a duke could survive without taking to an evening of fine brandy.

A copious amount of fine brandy.

Her words were gentle, but it was primarily what she said. In all of this, no one had even considered his feelings. As he thought of it, it *did* sound rather selfish. The poor girls had lost their parents and now were forced to deal with the likes of him. But still, it was a miserable adjustment for him, regardless of the fact that they'd be in Bath shortly. Before, all he had to worry about was his land, his title, and his person.

Now, he had the lives—the destinies—of three young women, and as much as he truly was the monster the *ton* gossiped about, he wasn't completely heartless. He took his job seriously, and those girls wouldn't go without a single necessity or want. He'd make sure of it.

He listened closely, waiting to see if she'd speak again.

"Yes, Miss Lottie. I suppose your right. Truly, we've not even met him yet. So it wouldn't be fair to judge him."

"At least yet," chimed in another voice.

Charles grimaced. He'd been avoiding them for a few days now, conveniently leaving before they were about and returning when he knew they wouldn't be awake. He truly had no idea what to say to them.

So he said nothing at all.

"I'm sure his grace is quite busy." The governess spoke again.

Was it his imagination or did her voice sound beautiful? Like it belonged to a beautiful woman, that was. He would know, he'd heard the voices of a great many women, many of them beautiful.

Curiosity captured his fancy and he decided that there was no time like the present, so he straightened his stature, tugged his gloves into place and took a deep breath. Pushing the door open, he was greeted by four gasps of surprise.

The young girls all looked remarkably alike, and strangely enough, reminded him of his mother's portrait of when she was younger. His eyes then moved to the governess.

And his mouth went dry.

He would have to have a very serious word with Mrs. Pott.

Mentally, he ran over his requirements for a governess for the girls. Appearance had never been spoken about, but in his head, he'd been thinking along the line of someone like…well, like Mrs. Pott.

Not the tempting beauty regarding him calmly. Calmly?

Shouldn't she be at the least mildly afraid? He was a duke after all, and his reputation did precede him. Surely, she knew, unless she was foreign?

"Hello, ladies." He bowed crisply then strode over to the head of the table.

Murray appeared in short order, filling his wine glass and setting a place for him.

"Your grace," the beauty replied, the girls echoing her voice in quick succession.

"I trust you are the new governess?" he asked.

"Yes, I was hired by your housekeeper just this morning," she replied, clearly not foreign but proper English.

"Very good, and you lovely ladies, must be the misses Lamonts."

"Yes, your grace," they murmured in unison.

"I'm pleased to make the acquaintance of such lovely ladies." He nodded, but his gaze slid over to the governess.

Her eyes narrowed slightly as if seeing through him.

Perhaps she did know his reputation then. No matter, in a few days' time, at the most, she would be gone to Bath with the girls, removing the temptation.

****

As his bloody luck would have it, it rained. Not the typical English spring shower, but a monsoon-like torrential downpour.

And after the first day, after he had tried to escape the confines of his house and ended up soaked before he made it to the second step, even with an umbrella, he decided he needed to catch up on his business.

By mid-afternoon, his eyes blurry and fully ready to direct themselves somewhere other than fine print, he strode out to the library.

And found it already occupied. Before he was noticed, he

began to close the door then paused.

"Miss Lottie? How do I waltz?" one of the girls asked, he assumed the oldest.

"Waltz? Well, first you should learn the cotillion, quadrille—"

"Oh! I know those! I just never... well we were *going* to learn the waltz next but..." Her voice trailed off, distinctly hesitant and... sad?

Belatedly he remembered the wards' loss of their parents. He knew the empty ache of loss that accompanied the death of one's mother and father, but he suspected that his wards had been far more attached to their parents than he had been to his.

"We shall remedy that, then." The governess spoke again her tone overly bright, as if she had heard the sorrow as well. *Carlotta.* He practiced the name in his mind, letting its cadence float to his lips in a whisper. It was a beautiful name, a passionate name. The sound of it evoked the idea of color and desire.

It was *not* the name for a governess, he decided, but a temptress.

Which was all too accurate.

A governess masquerading as a temptress. Heaven help him.

"Now, Beatrix? Can you play the pianoforte for us? Slowly, if you please."

"Yes, Miss Lottie."

"Bethanny, I'm going to lead. But first, you must know that before you waltz, you must have permission from a patroness of Almack's. Understood?"

"Yes, Miss Lottie."

"Now, then. My hand will hold your waist, and your hand will rest on my shoulder. Very good. Beatrix? If you will?"

The music began, painfully slow and all other instruction

given was unclear. Charles stood to leave, took a full step away from the door and then—

She laughed.

It was glorious sound, deep and rich, unabashed and unapologetic with a joy that came from deep within. It was artless, it was full, it was perfect.

Turning back around, he stared at the door, willing for the beautiful laughter to ring again.

He wasn't disappointed, and to his amazement, he felt himself grinning, then chuckling as he heard the other girls join in with the governess' amusement.

Unable to resist, he knocked.

Then entered, because well, it *was* his house.

"It seems that you are having entirely too joyful of a time in here," he said as he entered.

The music stopped.

The girls stood up straight.

The laughter…ended.

And his grin left at the same time.

"Is there a problem, your grace?" the governess, *Carlotta,* asked.

"No, no problem. I seem to be needed, however." He felt a roguish grin take the earlier one's place as a wicked thought entered his mind. "It seems that you are attempting to teach a waltz, am I correct?" he asked, walking forward.

"Yes, your grace," Carlotta responded, her eyebrows raised in curiosity.

"It is very difficult to learn unless observed first. Er…" He turned to the oldest girl, furrowing his brow as he tried to remember her name.

"Bethanny," Carlotta helped.

"Yes, Bethanny, have you ever seen a waltz?"

"Once, my parents showed me but it's been quite a while, your grace," she stammered, her cheeks high in color.

"Then allow me to assist." He turned towards Carlotta,

took three steps and held out his hands. "May I have the honor?" He bowed.

"Of—of, course, your grace."

Her cheeks were blooming with a delicate shade of rose, her eyes widening in surprise as she caught her lower lip in her teeth in what appeared to be a show of anxiety.

Glancing over to the piano player, he lifted his chin and then lowered it, signaling for her to begin.

He placed his hand at her waist, squeezing it slightly as he drew her in so that their bodies were separate by a respectable distance. A moment later, her hand rested on his shoulder, even as her gaze was firmly set on the location of his cravat. After grasping her hand and arching it out, he began to lead.

And all semblance this waltz had to a million others he had danced in his past ended in a breath. He had danced with a great many women in his day, but none of them compared with her.

His hand burned where it touched hers, causing the heat to crawl up his arm, burst through his chest and ignite a passion he would rather have remained hidden. The scent of lemon and lilac rose from her skin, inviting and fragrant and intoxicatingly alluring. Her steps were light, her body the perfect size and shape, the shape being all too close to the forefront of his mind as his hand rested on her waist.

He guided her through the steps, using the most subtle of cues for his direction and finding her flawlessly attentive. Her steps were graceful, and though her gaze hadn't lifted to his, he was shamelessly memorizing the heightened color of her cheeks, the delighted curve of her smile and her enjoyment made his complete.

Till she glanced up.

And he was reminded just how dangerous this dance could truly be. The music continued, reaching a crescendo that pulled him into the melody, and without forethought, he pulled her in tighter till he could feel her warmth.

Only when she stiffened and her gaze shifted back to his cravat did he realize what he was doing.

Only then did he remember that they had an audience.

A very *young* audience.

"That, Miss Bethanny, is how you waltz." He slowly released Carlotta as the music ended, his gaze never leaving her face. Then he lost himself in her green depths as her gaze rose to meet his.

"Oh," came Bethanny's breathless reply.

"Thank you, your grace." Carlotta curtseyed and, if he wasn't mistaken, her tone was deeper, husky... *affected*.

"The pleasure was mine." He bowed and then glanced away and into the faces of his three wards, all wearing very different expressions.

Bethanny's lips were split into an excited grin. The one on the piano, Beatrix? She was blushing as she averted her gaze and stacked her music and the youngest... Robert-something, started twirling with an invisible partner.

With a bow to the governess, he quit the room, his lips curving into a grin as he relived the sensation of her in his arms. But as soon as the delightful thoughts tumbled through his mind, he remembered her station.

And his.

And how foolish it was to entertain even the slightest attachment.

But bloody hell, if she wasn't perfection in his arms, then he didn't know what was.

****

"Let's have some tea, shall we girls?" Carlotta said as soon as the door closed behind the duke. She needed something, anything to distract her from the spell he had expertly woven around them while they danced.

If she'd ever doubted the rumors of his nature before, she believed them now. The man had practically turned the waltz into a ruining experience.

It was delicious.

And wrong. Very, very wrong.

He was her employer, and a *duke,* for heaven's sake! She could not let herself be affected by him.

She *would not* let him affect her.

"Miss Lottie! Do you think his grace will dance with me when I'm older?" Berty asked, her eyes wide with hope. "I've never seen anything so beautiful!" She sighed happily as she danced around the room, mimicking the waltz.

"Perhaps," Carlotta answered, her composure returning as she watched Berty twirl.

"He's a very good dancer," Beatrix commented as she stood from the piano. "You both are. I hope I'm as graceful as you, Miss Lottie," the girl added with a shy smile.

"I'm sure you'll be much more graceful than I, Beatrix," Carlotta answered with an answering grin.

"Is…I don't mean to question, Miss Lottie, but was that how *close* the waltz is?" Bethanny asked, her brow pinched.

Carlotta felt her face flush. "Not exactly, when you dance you'll want to maintain a bit more distance."

"Why?" Berty asked, pausing in her dance.

"For propriety's sake. The waltz is a very controversial dance, you see."

"Why?" she asked, again. Carlotta was discovering it was the child's favorite question.

"For many reasons, first, you are only with one partner not moving about like in a reel. Second, you are holding hands with the gentleman you are dancing with."

"Oh. That was my favorite part." Berty's shoulders slumped.

"If it's not proper though, why did you and the duke dance so close?" Beatrix asked, her eyes narrowing in confusion.

Carlotta opened her mouth to give some sort of reply, one she hadn't quite thought up yet, and was interrupted.

"Because... he's the duke and he may dance how he wants," Berty answered with a decisive nod.

"And there you have it." Carlotta nodded as well, thankful for the little girl's statement.

"Now, I believe I mentioned tea?" She spoke with a smile. Anything to get their little minds off the most beautiful waltz she'd ever experienced.

****

It was day four of the horrific rain. And Charles was feeling all the good will of a spring stag. He had finished all his paperwork, his estate business and anything else he could find. There was one final piece of business to which he had to attend.

He fingered the thick envelope then called for Murray.

"Yes, your grace?" Murray asked, his lean face emotionless.

"Please have this delivered to the address specified. Immediately."

"Very good, your grace." With a bow, he left.

It's done. Charles thought to himself, feeling a weight lifting off his shoulders.

He couldn't determine if it was the influence of having those wards in his home, or the allure of his pretty governess, but the thought of a mistress had turned decidedly sour.

It was an impulsive action, but one he didn't regret. Céline had been nothing if not gracious, but... the idea left him empty, hungering for something more, something deeper. Something he didn't quite understand or know how to attain but needed nonetheless. Taking the first step, he wrote the letter releasing her from his protection. No doubt she had quite a few gentlemen waiting for her availability. She'd have no worry about her welfare.

He felt lighter, somewhat confused at his rare inclination at emotion, but pleased nonetheless and so, with a somewhat sunnier disposition than the one with which he had begun the morning, he left his study and wandered down the hall.

And was immediately bored.

Blasted rain.

And, because he was curious and, indeed, he found it far too entertaining of a prospect, he wandered towards the nursery. He told himself it was *not* to see Carlotta, as had taken to calling her in his mind, but to check on the wards. They were his responsibility, after all.

He chose not to remember that just a few days ago he was wanting to ship them off to Bath without ever having to set eyes on them again.

So, with a blissfully ignorant decision made, he paused at the nursery door and waited. It was curiosity, he told himself. Nothing more. But he was spending an awful lot of time pressed against doors recently. He smiled wryly. To think, Charles Evermore, Duke of Clairmont, listening through doors. What had the world come to?

But as much as he tried to deny the truth, it didn't stick.

It was her voice. The soft melodic tones were full of life; unpretentious and free, they didn't have a sharp edge or double meaning. It was astoundingly refreshing, like an unexpected English rain shower just when one was overly warm from a long ride through the countryside. He hadn't even realized how jaded he'd become.

"Girls, wait here."

The words barely registered in Charles' mind before the door swung open, knocking him soundly on the forehead.

"Bloody—"

"What—oh! Your grace! Pardon me. I had... are you injured? Should I call for Murray?" Carlotta asked, her face etched in concern.

Charles studied her. Her eyes were wide with fear but also, concern. Her gaze roamed his features, no doubt searching for injuries. Her eyes focused on a point just above his brow.

"Your head." She spoke softly, then reaching out she placed the softest touch to his forehead, grazing his skin before her eyes widened as if realizing just what she was doing.

"I'm so sorry, forgive me."

"Nothing to forgive." Charles nodded, but his body was still humming from her gentle touch. Like a shock, only infinitely more pleasurable, her touch had created the softest glow of warmth that started at his head and traveled through the rest of his body, slowly growing into the familiar burning of desire.

He swallowed. Now was not the time to think about bedding the help. Come to think of it, it wasn't *ever* a good time to think of bedding the help.

"Was there something you needed?" Carlotta asked, her face still concerned.

Wrong question, because he could think of a great many things he… needed.

"I'm quite well. Just a… bump." He winced as he touched the tender place on his forehead.

"Again, I'm so sorry."

"There's no need."

Carlotta nodded, and turned to go back into the temporary nursery.

"Wasn't there something *you* needed, Miss Standhope?" Charles asked smoothly, inwardly grinning that she was so flustered.

"Oh, yes. I'm needing, well, my hair pins actually." She glance downward, a humble smile teasing her lips.

Her very pink and delicious looking lips.

"Hair pins?" His curiosity completely piqued, he crossed

his arms and waited for her to explain.

"Yes, it's a game of sorts."

"Very well, don't let me stop you."

She bobbed a curtsey and left.

He thought about leaving too, but found himself too curious.

She returned shortly, and paused in walking through the door as her gaze rested upon him, sitting in a chair. He grinned at her expectantly.

"His grace wishes to play too!" Berty exclaimed, her face lighting up in a cheerful smile.

"My, well, I'm sure his grace will at least find our game diverting." She spoke hesitantly as if she didn't quite believe the words she was speaking, but said them nonetheless.

She laid out several pins, most of which were open in the shape of a 'V'.

"This is how we play. Everyone select a pin."

Everyone did, including Charles. He lifted his hand to cover his lips to prevent his grin from breaking through at the color blooming to his governess' cheeks. The enticing shade of pink only heightened her beauty, causing his grin to falter. Forcing his thoughts back to the game, he cleared his throat, earning a questioning glanced from the object of his desire.

She regarded him then continued explaining. "Now, I'll place the rest of the pins on the table in a heap. Using your own pin, you must try to remove as many pins from the heap without moving any others, save the one you're trying to remove. If you jostle the pile or move a pin other than the one you intended, your turn is over and the next person has a chance. The person with the most hair pins wins."

"I think I remember a game like this, but I don't remember stealing my mother's pins to play it." He spoke conspiratorially as he leaned slightly towards her. The air around her was fragrant, reminding him of lemons and honey. He inhaled deeply. Why couldn't there be something about her that didn't lure him? Why couldn't she have smelled like damp clothing or boiled cabbage?

She stiffened as he lingered near her. "I'm improvising." She spoke wryly.

Charles couldn't suppress a grin.

The girls took their turns. Beatrix collected four pins, Bethanny secured six before moving the heap and thus losing her turn. Berty's little pink tongue stuck out while she made a valiant effort to get two. Then it was Charles' turn.

He studied the pile and began to select pins, withdrawing them one by one with practiced care. He collected ten, leaving only four on the table. He leaned back, raising a challenging brow to Carlotta, daring her to beat him.

"Miss Lottie! We haven't enough pins!" cried Beatrix.

"I should have brought more back, but it's no matter. His grace is the winner." She offered him a bright smile.

Charles tried to ignore the stab of desire her beautiful expression gave him. "Miss Lottie," he crooned, watching her eyes narrow slightly at the use of her shortened name. "I insist you try to beat my record. After all, I hate winning without a fair game."

"I haven't any more pins..." she replied, then paused as Charles gave a pointed look at her hair.

"I can't very well take down my hair, your grace," she replied, a bit of an edge to her tone.

Good, thought Charles, it was best if she had more of a prickly demeanor around him. It might remind him that he wasn't interested.

Because he wasn't.

At least that's what he was telling himself that very moment. Though his body and mind weren't in accord.

"Why ever not?" he asked casually, biting back a smirk at the annoyed glint in her eyes.

"Because," she spoke carefully, though her eyes were flashing green fire. "I'm to train the girls in the way of proper society. A lady does not unbind her hair in the company of gentlemen."

"Why not?" Berty asked.

"Yes, Miss Lottie. Why not?" Charles repeated the child's question. At Carlotta's disbelieving expression, he began to chuckle, earning him a glare.

"It, er, well it gives to much of a feeling of… intimacy." She blushed to the roots of her hair.

"But it's just us! And the duke, but he's old, Miss Lottie," Berty quipped.

Charles choked and began to cough. Old! She thought he was old? Well, compared to a seven-year-old, he supposed he was…older. The idea of being old chafed him, yet it played into his little plan quite well.

"Er, yes, Miss Lottie. I'm quite ancient. Therefore, not a threat." He grinned wolfishly.

"You are quite… *advanced* in your years," she returned, her eyebrow arching.

That stung more than Charles would let on. Ever.

With a defiant gleam in her eye, she began to pull out her pins.

One by one.

If she were an opera singer, he would swear it she did it as a ploy. But he was convinced of her thorough innocence, at least in that aspect. After all, no ruined woman would blush as easily as she. But as she took out each pin, Charles found himself unable to even swallow. Her hair tumbled down gently, curling and waving over her shoulders in a golden halo.

And the fragrance.

It was lemon and lavender, intertwined with a fresh scent he had no name for but knew was unique to her. It was far more potent than when he had leaned in earlier. Its potency was almost his undoing.

At last, the final pin was removed and she shook her

head gently, letting the entirety of her beautiful mane settle.

Charles finally was able to swallow, but his mouth was dry. If he ever needed brandy, it was now. The ploy to tease had indeed turned on him.

With a small smile, she put the pins in a pile, equaling fourteen in all.

Grinning she began to extract them one by one till none remained.

"I believe you won, Miss Lottie."

"I believe I did."

Chapter Three

"Lord Graham to see you, your grace," Murray informed Charles.

"See him in, of course."

"Yes, your grace." Murray left; the soft clicking of the door was the only sound, save a few crackles of the fire as it glowed in the hearth in his study.

Charles had been lost in his own thoughts. Ever since that ridiculous hairpin game yesterday, he hadn't been able to cease thinking about Carlotta Standhope. Of course, if he were honest with himself, he would have included that he'd been having a rather hard time not thinking about her even before the hairpin game. But he wasn't being honest with himself. He rather liked living in denial. It seemed far simpler. After all, when one admitted to attraction, so many more emotions and questions arose.

"Clairmont!" Edward Greenly, Earl of Graham walked into the study with the ease of someone familiar with the room. After all, he had been Charles' chum since their days at Eton. Friend, partner in crime, really it was all the same.

"Graham. What brings you here this wet morning?"

Charles grinned at his friend. Graham was the kind of bloke one simply had to smile around. His deep dimples on his face had cause many a woman to swoon. Though he cursed them as a young boy, he now found them supremely helpful when consorting amongst the *ton*.

His reputation wasn't nearly as black as Charles', though he was known for his much quieter exploits. But rather than make him unapproachable, it somehow endeared him even more to the matchmaking mommas of the *ton*. For that reason, he hadn't attended an evening party for quite some time, at least not one his sister hadn't required him to attend. Which was self-preservation in both instances. To abstain meant freedom from the matchmaking and scheming mothers, and attending, when required, allowed him peace from his harridan of a sister. Lady Southridge was a formidable force not to be reckoned with. At fourteen years Graham's senior, she was more of a mother than a sister, especially since both of their parents had perished while he was quite young.

"I'm leaving for Scotland on the morrow and thought I'd stop to say goodbye. It's come to my attention that my estate is requiring my presence."

"Ah, the one near Edinburg?"

"Precisely."

"Well, I wish you well."

"Of course you do. But in the meantime, can you please tell my sister where I'll be?"

"No."

"Please? You know if I tell her I'll have to attend one final ball before I go and I'm not up to it."

"Bloody hell you're not. You're just wanting to avoid her schemes."

"Yes. I'm man enough to admit that I'm running away."

"I fail to see how that amounts to being a man," Charles retorted sarcastically, earning an unrepentant grin from Graham.

"So you'll tell her?"

"No. In fact I believe I already said that."

"I can always send a letter..." Graham mumbled as he sat in a damask chair facing the fire. He rubbed his chin absentmindedly.

"Yes, that will go over nicely. You know she'll just redouble her efforts to marry you off or, heaven forbid, she'll follow you to Scotland."

"Bloody hell, do you think she would?" Graham's gaze was horror-stricken.

"The better question is, do *you* think she would?" Charles raised his eyebrows and waited, rocking on his heels.

"Damn."

"I thought as much."

"Please Clairmont, you're my only hope." Graham stood and faced his friend, his amber colored eyes imploring.

"I'm not your mistress. You can't beg or charm your way into my good graces."

Graham sighed heavily.

Charles turned towards the door at the sound of children's voices. Closing his eyes, he prayed they would cease. He hadn't told a soul about his position as ward over the girls, or the governess he had employed. The last thing he wanted was to infuse London society with fresh gossip.

"I say Charles, do you have company?"

"Fifteen, sixteen, seventeen, eighteen, nineteen, twenty! Here I come!"

"Bloody hell," Charles swore.

"Clairmont?" Graham asked.

Just then, the door to his study swung open and in ran Berty, frantically looking for a place to hide. She had shut the door and taken two steps before she froze, her eyes wide with surprise, then fear.

"I-I—forgive me, your grace. I-I—"

"Berty." Charles spoke in a clipped tone. "Would you

please abstain from using my study as a hiding place in the future?"

"Y-yes your grace."

"Thank you. Now—"

"Berty?" Beatrix opened the door and peeked in, searching for her sister. As her gaze met Charles', the grin she wore faded into a repentant expression full of guilt.

"Hello Beatrix. Your sister is right here." Charles sighed heavily. All that was left to do was wait for Bethanny. Where was the governess? Wasn't this why he'd hired her? To keep the girls from interrupting his life? This certainly qualified as an interruption.

"Hello, your grace," Beatrix mumbled and stood, placing her hands behind her back. Berty scrambled over to her sister, standing slightly behind her as if still afraid.

"I give up! Where are—oh." Bethanny's cheeks flushed crimson and she nodded to Charles and Graham. "Your grace, sir. Um, please forgive us for interrupting—"

The sound of the clipping of heels on the marbled hall floor had all three girls glancing to the hall, then to Charles. Three varying degrees of guilt apparent on their faces as they waited for Miss Lottie's arrival.

Charles simply held his breath. Not only had he withheld himself from the governess' company since their little game yesterday, but also, he didn't want Graham to suspect his feelings. Truly, it was turning in to a nightmare of a morning.

"Girls?" Carlotta's voice was soft, as if she were trying to be as quiet as possible while still calling for her errant charges.

The sound of her footsteps stopped just in front of the slightly ajar door. She seemed to pause, and then the door opened slowly. "Girls?"

"Do come in, Miss Lottie. We're having quite the party," Charles said dryly.

Carlotta's face flamed with a blush that was likely equal parts humiliation and anger towards the girls. "Forgive us, your grace. We'll take our leave now." Carlotta nodded then turned an icy glare to the girls.

"Clairmont? Are you going to introduce me?" Graham asked smoothly. Charles glanced over to his friend and narrowed his eyes. Graham was grinning, showing off his blasted dimples as he approached Carlotta. His stride was overly confident and immediately Charles felt the fiery stab of jealousy. His jaw clenched as a strongly possessive nature overwhelmed him. Taking a deep breath, lest his friend see his rampaging emotions, he swallowed the scathing retorts he wanted to say.

"Graham, allow me to introduce you to my three wards and their governess, Miss Carlotta Standhope." He clenched his jaw afterward as he watched Graham take Carlotta's hand and caress it flirtatiously before kissing the air above her wrist.

"A pleasure, Miss Standhope."

"Thank you." Carlotta spoke demurely. Her gaze met Charles', and he lost himself momentarily in the depths of her eyes before she glanced to Graham, then back to him as if asking a question.

"Where are my manners? Miss Lottie..." He smirked as she slightly narrowed her eyes at his familiar manner. "This is Lord Graham."

"A pleasure, Lord Graham."

"I find that the pleasure is all mine, Miss Carlotta. Or is it Miss Lottie?" Graham grinned wickedly.

"Carlotta, if you please."

"Of course."

"And, who may I ask are these beautiful angels?" Graham turned to face the three girls."

"These little angels—" Charles cleared his throat meaningfully. "—are Roberta, Beatrix and Bethanny."

All of the girls smiled shyly at Graham, save Berty who was glaring at Charles at his use of her formal name. But to her credit, she didn't correct him.

"A pleasure to meet you lovely ladies."

"A pleasure to meet you, your grace," the girls echoed in unison. Bethanny was blushing profusely at Graham's attentions, causing Charles to experience a strange sensation clenching his stomach. The poor girl was too young and innocent to be charmed by the likes of his friend. Quickly he interceded before she could get any ideas in her young mind concerning his rake of a friend.

"Miss Carlotta, would you please escort the girls to the school room?" Charles clipped more than he had intended.

Carlotta nodded and ushered the girls out. "Please accept my apologies, your grace." She spoke with a quiet dignity as she was about to leave.

"Your apology is accepted."

With a slight nod, she followed the girls from the room and closed the door.

Charles watched the door close, tamping down the urge to call her back in and see her just once more. But no, he needed to detach himself, keep her out of his mind before she wormed her way into his heart. She would be leaving with the girls in a few days; he'd likely not seem them for months, maybe even years. And aside from that, dukes did not consort with the help. Regardless of how beautiful they may be.

"Clairmont? I say old chap, are you with me?" Graham walked into Charles' line of sight and broke him from his musings.

"What?"

"I've been asking you when you were saddled with three wards for the past few minutes. All you've been doing is staring at the door as if you saw a bloody ghost."

"Yes, well. It turns out I'm their nearest relative so I inherited the little monsters when their parents perished."

"You, with three girl wards? Hell must have frozen over."

"Precisely my thoughts. That and heaven's hysterical

laughter."

"That too, I imagine." Graham nodded sagely.

"And what do you plan to do with them? I see you've secured a governess. Though how you found one so... bewitching, I'll never know. Some have all the luck."

"Yes, being saddled with three young girls as wards certainly certifies my lucky state," Charles replied sarcastically.

"I'd say a governess like that is far more lucky than having three wards is unlucky. But that's just my opinion."

"I don't consort with the help, Graham."

"Of course not, but you can certainly enjoy a beautiful view, can you not?"

"We're done discussing this."

"Fine, but... when did you become their guardian? I've yet to hear about it in town and if I, your friend, had no idea..." His voice trailed off as he seemed to gain understanding. "You don't want anyone to know."

"No. Can you imagine the gossips?"

"It would be a veritable feeding frenzy."

"Quite right."

"So..." Graham's face twisted into an evil grin, one that Charles knew all too well from their prankster days.

"Heaven help me," Charles mumbled.

"Indeed. So, in payment for my silence concerning your little sweet dessert of a governess and three wards, you'll tell my sister of my departure for Scotland. After all, it's only a fair trade you see."

"Bloody hell. Why are you my friend?"

"Because I'm the only one able to outwit a duke."

"Don't flatter yourself."

"So are we agreed?"

"Agreed. But if word gets out and I find that you were the source, I'll help your sister, and make sure you're caught in a compromising position with some unsavory wench.

Agreed?"

"There's no need to be vindictive," Graham grumbled.

"Just a little insurance, you understand."

Graham sighed heavily. "Agreed. Who knows, maybe I'll be a prince from that cinder story and redeem the lovely servant girl from the wicked duke's employ." Charles wagged his eyebrows.

"You nodcock, first it was a stepmother, not a wicked duke, and you, my friend, are no prince."

"I've been told I look like one." Charles performed a mocking bow, grinning like a fool.

"That was one drunk tavern wench. So it does not count. Plus, with Prinny as the only prince we know, I'd not say that you are complimenting yourself, especially with his girth."

"I'll make sure I tell him that at Carlton house."

"You'll do no such thing."

"You're right of course, but I might consider rescuing the damsel."

"From my evil ways?"

"You of all people know how evil they truly are."

"Not in this case. I assure you I'm the paragon of virtue." Charles spoke confidently, though his own heart called him a liar.

"I don't believe you for a moment, but if you want to pretend your mouth wasn't watering at the delicious sight that little governess presented, then you go ahead and pretend."

"Aren't you leaving the country tomorrow and have errands to do? I believe you said you were in a hurry..." Charles suggested.

"Have all the time in the world, maybe I'll postpone my trip."

"Lady Southridge." Charles spoke her name and watched Graham's eyes narrow.

"You know, I do have somewhere to be."

"I thought as much."

"Try not to get into too much trouble while I'm gone."

"Because you're the one who would rescue me? Is that it?"

"I always do. I'll see you upon my return, Clairmont." Graham chuckled and waved as quit the room.

"Upon your return." Charles grinned at his friend as he left.

Chapter Four

"How could you girls?" Carlotta tried to rein in her tempter as she saw each girl glance down onto her lap with a guilt-ridden expression. Never had she been so humiliated. Not only did she seem incompetent in front of her employer, but also his guest! She hoped it wouldn't affect her employment; she'd never get a good reference if she were dismissed so shortly after being hired. Then what would she do?

"We're sorry, Miss Lottie. It was my fault. I kept pestering them to play with me. I knew you were busy setting up our picnic lunch with cook and I got so bored," Berty explained.

"I was gone for ten minutes, Berty."

"Ten minutes is a long time," Berty whined, her rosebud lips pouting.

"We knew better Miss Lottie, but well... we haven't seen much of the house and thought it would be a good way to explore," Beatrix explained, her tone apologetic.

"I see. And you, Bethanny? What is your excuse?" Carlotta asked, her anger dissipating.

"Berty has always loved playing hide and seek. She was so happy once she thought of the idea to play I didn't want to let her down. We... we have a hard time smiling still, Miss Lottie." Bethanny's voice dropped to a whisper. "After everything...you know."

Carlotta's heart broke. Truly, the girls were doing well, so well it was easy to forget that they were suffering and mourning. Children were able to bounce back from tragedy quicker than adults, at least that was what she always thought. But that didn't mean they didn't hurt. She knew too well the pain they endured.

"I see." Carlotta nodded then paused to take in a calming breath. "I understand, but I cannot approve."

"Yes, Miss Lottie," Bethanny responded, followed by her two sisters' echoes of repentance.

"The duke, while he is your guardian, is not to be disturbed. He is an important man with responsibilities that need his attention. This house, it is his home and we must respect his need and desire for privacy. If there is a room that you've not been in, you should not enter it unless invited. This is simply being polite. Do you understand?"

"Yes, Miss Lottie," they echoed.

"Very well. Now then." Carlotta smoothed her skirts. "I believe now would be a brilliant time to take our picnic."

"Truly? We may still go?" Beatrix asked, her face lit up with hope.

"I said I'd take you, and I shall. We are quite close to Hyde Park. The fresh air shall do us all a world of good."

"Thank you! Thank you! Thank you, Miss Lottie! You are truly the best!" Berty exclaimed and rushed forward, hugging Carlotta's waist in an excited grasp.

"You're welcome." Carlotta grinned at the girls. Their smiles were slowly returning and she hoped that the duke would overlook her incompetence so that she could watch their smiles return to their full brightness. Truly, she had no deeper desire than that.

But if he didn't, if she were dismissed, then she would make the last memory she had with the girls one to remember.

****

"Mrs. Pott? Where is our little governess?" Charles asked, his temper only barely in check. He had asked Murray, a few maids and now the housekeeper in an attempt to locate the errant governess and his patience was running thin. Already he was testy from the previous incident leaving him in a wretched position with Lady Southridge. Not wanting to dwell on the miserable errand he was committed to doing, he wrote the damnable letter and gave Murray strict instructions to deliver it in the morning. Surely, that would give Graham enough time to escape his overbearing sister.

"I've not seen her for quite some time, your grace. But I know she was talking with Cook…"

"Cook? Would you please ask Cook if she has any information on her whereabouts?" Charles asked with clenched teeth. Was it truly that difficult to locate someone within his own home?

"Of course, your grace. I'll be but a moment."

Mrs. Pott left, leaving Charles brooding in the library. His anger over the girls' interruption had dissipated, but with the inability to locate them or the governess, he found himself in a temper again.

"Your grace?" Mrs. Pott entered the library once more.

"Yes?"

"Miss Carlotta took the girls on a picnic in Hyde Park. They left a little over an hour ago."

"Thank you."

"Of course…" Mrs. Pott was hesitant, her expression concerned.

"Is there something more?" Charles asked tiredly.

"Well, your grace, I'm simply concerned about the children. The weather has gotten ever so severe since their departure and I'm—"

"What do you mean?" Charles growled then turned to a window. Sliding open the drapes he saw what his housekeeper meant. The blue skies of earlier that day were gone, replaced with an ominous and heavy cloud cover that was proceeding to gush water from the heavens. A stiff breeze rocked the window glass, causing it to shudder.

"Bloody hell. Get Murray!" Charles called.

Mrs. Pott didn't respond, simply rushed out as fast as her plump body could carry her. A few moments later Murray arrived.

"Your grace?"

"I'll need my greatcoat, and have my mount saddled."

"Pardon, your grace, but wouldn't you prefer the closed carriage in this weather?"

Charles paused. The carriage would be slower, but infinitely wiser. When he did locate the girls and governess, he'd not be able to do much on his mount, however a carriage could easily take them all back.

"Very well."

"As you wish." Murray exited quickly, clearly tuned in to the impatience in the duke's voice.

"Just what was the chit thinking in taking those girls out in this weather?" He grumbled to himself. Though he knew the answer. English weather was unpredictable at best. It could have easily been beautiful an hour ago. With the many buildings and being so near the park, the trees also inhibited a view of the skyline, causing one to easily misjudge the conditions. Often a rain-filled cloud was just beyond the line of sight. But surely she could have made her way home after the first few raindrops!

"Here, your grace." Murray came in the library with Charles' greatcoat, gloves, and hat. After quickly donning them, he rushed out into the hall and out the front door to his awaiting carriage. The springs rocked under his weight as he entered into the cab and waited for the driver to urge the horses forward.

The *clip clop* of the matched bays' shoes sounded on the cobbled streets of Mayfair, and soon the large park was in sight. Rotten Row was deserted, puddles of mud making it not only dangerous but also filthy for the next few days. The rain veritably pounded on the roof of the carriage and made visibility short sighted. The heavy cloying fragrance of rain and humidity hung in the air, making it thick.

After taking several paths, he tapped on the roof, causing the driver to halt the horses. There just under a weeping beech, or upside down tree, stood four women clustered together.

"Damn females," Charles swore and opened the carriage door. Immediately he was in the deluge of rainwater and quickly became soaked to the skin.

He half jogged, half walked across the ground, his boots sinking in the soggy grass. As he reached the tree, he held out his hand to the soaked girls and sodden governess.

"Don't just stand there! Let's get going before we all catch our death!" Charles shouted.

Not needing any more encouragement, all four ladies ran to the closed carriage and tumbled in. Charles followed suit. Once all were seated, the carriage moved forward towards his home.

"Would anyone care to tell me whose brilliant idea it was to have a picnic in the park?" Charles asked as a rivulet of water trickled down his nose and dripped off, landing on his folded hands.

The girls all glanced to the floor, their little bodies shivering from cold and wet. Charles had an unfamiliar pang of sympathy.

"It was mine, your grace," Carlotta replied, her head held high and jaw clenched in defiance. Or perhaps it was clenched in cold.

"I see. That wasn't your most brilliant of plans, Miss Lottie." Charles' words were light, but his tone was menacing.

"I would think that quite apparent, your grace," Carlotta replied curtly.

Good. Thought Charles. Let her be upset, let her feel the frustration she'd caused him earlier! He glared at Carlotta.

"Thank you, your grace." Berty's unusually quiet voice broke through his vindictive musings.

"Oh, well. Of course…" Charles responded, his brow creasing.

"Yes, thank you, your grace," Bethanny and Beatrix murmured together, they glanced up then dropped their gazes once more.

At once, the anger burning in Charles' chest was doused like a fire caught in the rain. Unable to resist baiting his pretty governess, he allowed a mischievous grin to twist his lips. Raising his eyebrows expectantly, he tilted his head as he held her steady gaze, waiting for her gratitude as well.

"Yes. Thank you," Carlotta obliged him, her cheeks flushed with a deep crimson, and he fancied that it was more from his expectant behavior and arrogant nature than true gratitude.

"It's of no matter. We'll be back shortly and I'll have Mrs. Pott bring you some hot tea."

"Thank you, your grace." Carlotta spoke again, this time her tone was softer, full of gratitude.

Charles turned his gaze back towards her. She offered him a repentant smile then lowered her gaze to her lap, studying her soiled and sodden gloves as she fidgeted.

Her lashes were spiked from the rain, making them darker and fuller against the pale glow of her skin. She worried her lower lip, causing it to bloom in richer color, heightening its allure and plumping it further. Charles bit back a groan at the sight she presented. Surely, she was more alluring in even the most unbecoming of circumstances. Shaking his head, he turned his gaze towards the girls.

Bethanny had been watching him, a curious expression on her face. Her curious gaze shifted from him, to Carlotta, then back, her expression full of questions.

Charles cleared his throat, uncomfortable with the young lady's awareness. "Bethanny, will you please see to your sisters while I speak with your governess?" He asked, hoping to eliminate any conclusions the girl might draw between himself and the governess.

"Y-yes your grace," she stammered, her wide eyes darting between him and Carlotta, fear evident in her gaze.

"Thank you." He nodded then turned to Carlotta.

Her eyes were still downcast, her body slightly trembling. Was she that cold? At once Charles was concerned. After all, he didn't want to be bothered with finding a new governess.

Though he'd never been bothered with finding one in the first place.

However, he refused to dwell on that lie and rather accept it as truth. Denial being simpler and all that.

They arrived at his town residence and after a footman opened the door, they exited. Charles waited until the ladies had stepped out before he did so himself. He straightened his greatcoat, and bounded up the steps, entering into the warmth of his home. Bethanny and the two younger girls paused then made their way to their rooms.

"Girls! I was so worried! Let's get you dried off and I'll have some hot tea and biscuits for you. Come along." Mrs. Pott appeared from down the hall and ushered the girls along like an old hen with her chicks.

Charles couldn't help a small grin at the sight.

"Your grace?" Carlotta's soft query reminded him that he had intended to speak with her.

"Follow me." He didn't turn but strode to his study. The

clicking of her heels on the marble hall floor notified him that she was indeed following behind. He opened the thick wooden door and waited for her to enter the study. Squaring his shoulders, he followed, closing it firmly behind him.

He saw her glance to the closed door then back to him, her eyes slightly panicked, though to her credit, she didn't say a word.

Charles didn't know if that meant she was afraid or if she thought he was a threat to her reputation. Neither idea sat well with him.

"Miss Lottie, I'm sure you're aware of why we are having this conversation," he began as he made his way to the crackling fire.

"Yes, your grace. My sincerest apologies. I'll simply pack and be—"

"Pack? What ever for?" Charles turned, scowling.

"Am I not dismissed?" she asked, her voice trembling.

Charles took a moment to study her. Her dress was soaked, as was her pelisse. Her gloves were ruined and the once tidy, if not far too strict, bun on the nape of her neck was dripping. In fact, between her hair and clothes, a puddle had begun to form at her feet.

"Bloody hell," Charles cursed, earning a gasp from Carlotta. Oh well, let her feminine sensibilities be offended. He wasn't the least bit repentant. Angry at himself for not noticing her soaked state, he glanced about for a blanket or something to aid her. What was she thinking? Not asking for a moment to refresh herself! Though he doubted she felt the freedom to ask such a thing, he still wished she would have!

"Here." Charles shrugged out of his greatcoat, at a loss for finding anything else.

Carlotta's eyes widened, but she obeyed and slipped her arms into the coat as he held it out for her.

He pulled it over her shoulders, settling it. Tugging on the lapels, he tugged her forward and towards the fire. As he did, he felt how her body was shivering and saw the telltale trembling of her jaw. But not once did she complain.

What type of woman didn't complain?

She simply stood before the fire, holding out her sodden gloved hands and shivered.

"Take off your gloves for pity's sake," Charles grumbled and reached for her hands.

"But—"

"No arguing. You'll never warm up with wet gloves." Though as soon as the words flew from his mouth he bit back a groan. Wet gloves were the least of her worries when her entire dress was dripping on the floor.

"Thank you," she said with quiet grace.

"You're welcome. Now. I'll not have you think I'm dismissing you. To be sure I'm not keen on the fact that I was interrupted not once but four times this afternoon, but that's no bloody reason to gallivant about the city and get soaked."

Carlotta's lips thinned into a irritated line as she as she glanced to him after his speech. "I wasn't gallivanting about town."

"Oh, and what exactly do you call, whatever it was you were doing?" Charles asked, crossing his arms.

"Having a picnic," she said dryly.

"In the rain?"

"It wasn't raining when we left." She spoke through clenched teeth.

"Have you no understanding of London weather? Just because it's not raining doesn't mean it's going to stay that way! One must always assume it will rain at some point." Charles huffed indignantly. Just where had the girl grown up if not London? As he thought the question, he realized just how little he knew about Carlotta. A strange prickling in his chest made him realize how much he resented that fact. He wanted to know about her.

Nothing could have scared him more.

"I'll keep that useful information in mind," Carlotta retorted.

"Very well," Charles responded weakly, still rocked by his realization of the depth of his emotional involvement.

His *futile* emotional involvement.

Of course, that didn't seem to be stopping him from being captivated by her lips.

Her green eyes reflected the firelight, giving them an orange halo in the center. Luscious lips parted as her pink tongue caressed her lower lip before biting it.

Charles bit back a groan. The minx wasn't even trying, and she was fully seducing him.

Without thinking, because had he *thought*, he certainly wouldn't have *acted*, he took the two steps towards her, which brought them nose-to-nose. Her eyes widened, but she didn't back away. Which was all the invitation Charles needed.

Slowly, he lowered his head, caressing her face with his gaze until the last moment when he allowed his eyes to slip closed. A fraction of a second later, he felt the soft pillowy bliss of her lips touching his. Her breath was sweet, warm and inviting, so he kissed her again, lingering a moment longer. When she didn't move, he reached out and placed his hands on her shoulders, encouraging her as his lips caressed hers once more, teasing them, tasting them and tutoring them to accept his attentions. The fragrance of cedar and fresh rain mingled around her, adding to the heightened awareness that had already woven a spell over him.

Tentatively, she kissed him back.

****

Certainly, Carlotta had thought about what it would be like to be kissed. But not ever having experienced it personally, her imagination could only be so creative in its daydreaming.

Nothing could have ever prepared her for what the real experience held.

Never could she have imagined the softness of a man's lips, not when his frame was so muscled and hard. Never would she have guessed a kiss could be gentle and not chaste. The heat from his hands as they rested on her shoulders surely anchored her to the spot, a delicious weight that added to the already heady pleasure of the kiss.

A kiss she was beginning to return. At first, she was so shocked, she was quite frozen, even keeping her eyes open as he gave the first kiss. But slowly, as his warm mouth teased hers, offering her gentle coaching, she found herself wanting—no, needing—to return the kiss. She mimicked his movements, the flick of his tongue and the nibbling of his lips till she heard him groan softly. He deepened the kiss, surprising her once more with the *pleasure* of it.

His tongue tickled her lower lip, breaking the seal of her own lips and caressing the edge of her teeth.

Never once had she imagined a tongue being part of a kiss.

For now on, she'd not be able to imagine a kiss without one.

Her heart beat wildly, surely pounding hard enough for the duke to feel, pressed up against as tightly as she was. Absentmindedly, she wondered when that had happened. But as he softly broke the seal of their lips, she found she didn't care. He drew back slightly, his eyes cloudy with… passion? Was that what it looked like on a man? It was deliriously delicious, and she wondered if she looked the same. His eyes, so light normally, had darkened. His irises were wide giving his gaze a smoldering quality that burned her from the inside out. His lips were still slightly wet from their exchange. She gazed at them, wondering at their softness.

She waited, not wanting to move but also not knowing what to say. What did one say after a kiss? The duke seemed to be facing the same dilemma for he made no movement and spoke no words, simply gazed at her as if seeing her for the first time.

"I...I..." he whispered, his soft breath fanning across her face.

She swallowed. Somehow, feeling like his next words would be pivotal.

"You should dry off." He stepped back and nodded, turning to the fire, effectively dismissing her.

"Oh, y-yes, your grace," Carlotta stammered, her confusion and the sting of rejection painful in her breast. Before the tears that were welling in her eyes slipped out, she turned and left with as much dignity as she could muster.

A kiss that had tilted her world and branded her heart seemed to have had no effect whatsoever on the duke.

And nothing could have hurt more.

Chapter Five

Charles stared at the fire until he heard the soft click of her heels in the hall, then he closed his eyes in shame. What a miserable emotion! What a miserable situation he found himself in, over a governess no less.

But if he were being honest, and he found that he was, indeed, being honest, she wasn't *just* a governess any longer. Not after that kiss.

Charles considered himself experienced in the more romantic arts, to say the least. He was familiar with all types of kisses; seductive kisses meant to lure a man to bed, as well as flirtatious kisses, meant to entice but innocent enough to simply tease. But one kiss he was not familiar with was an inexperienced kiss. Contrary to what he would have assumed, it was by far the most tempting, alluring siren call of all.

Or perhaps it was just *her* kiss.

She had tasted of sweet strawberries and cream, all smooth and velvety. Her lips were far softer than he expected, captivating him from the first whisper of contact. Her tentative response was nearly his undoing if it hadn't reminded him of her purity, of her innocent nature regarding seduction.

If her innocence was as captivating as that, then heaven help the man with whom she discovered her passions.

Charles swallowed hard. *He* wanted to be that man. The thought of any other man teaching her the joys of passion made his blood boil with a fever of rage.

Normally he wasn't one given to extreme emotions, yet she seemed to provoke a great many within him. Just another aspect of the decadence that was his governess.

His *governess*.

As if he needed a reminder of the difference in their stations, he glanced down to his ring; the family ring that had carried though generations and generations of Clarimonts. Not once had there been a marriage that didn't include the purest of pedigrees.

A governess. His father must be spinning in his grave. Charles shook his head, trying to dispel the conflicting and confusing emotions and thoughts.

This was why he chose to live in denial. Too bad that ship had apparently sailed away, along with his sanity.

What had he been thinking to kiss her like that? Dripping wet no less, he had practically accosted her. Only, she hadn't run away. She'd kissed him back.

She had *kissed* him back.

Startled by the obvious realization, he felt a self-satisfied grin overtake his features. It was short lived as he remembered just how he ended the lovely exchange of a kiss.

Yes, shame overcame him again.

Would the carousel of emotions ever end? It was bloody exhausting, all this caring and wondering. Yet at the same time, it was blissful and exhilarating. Women chased *him*, where now he would be the one to pursue, if he did, indeed, choose to pursue.

But he couldn't.

She was, after all, a governess. Probably from a merchant family, blue stocking to the core.

But that kiss made him almost willing to take the chance. Almost.

****

"Miss Lottie?" Berty asked as they sat down to dinner in the smaller dining room decorated in deep sapphire blues.

"Yes, Berty?" Carlotta smiled at the girl, though her heart still ached. What had she been thinking? Kissing a duke? Therein lay the problem, she *hadn't* been thinking. She was consoled with the idea that apparently, he hadn't been thinking either.

Unless.

Carlotta's skin erupted in goose bumps, not the pleasant kind either. Surely the duke didn't think she was a light skirt! One that would dally with her employer? Humiliation at her naïveté washed through her, soaking her soul like the rain had soaked her dress earlier. Was that all it was? Was she simply... available? Yet, if the rumors were true, then he needed not search out feminine companionship. It sought *him* out...

"Miss Lottie?" Bethanny asked.

"Yes?"

"Are you well?" All three girls were watching her with various degrees of concern etching their beautiful faces.

"Forgive me, I was woolgathering." Carlotta flushed at being so absorbed in her own misery that she frightened the girls. "What were you saying, Berty?"

"I was asking... that is, you're still our governess, aren't you? The duke, he wasn't too mad at you for the picnic?" Berty asked, her question uncharacteristically observant.

"I'm still your governess. The duke spoke with me—" She swallowed, remembering far more than his words. "But have no fear, I'm not dismissed."

"Good." Beatrix nodded. "It wasn't your fault anyway."

"In a way, it is my dears. I'm to train you but also keep a

sharp eye on you. I failed that charge."

"But we all but ran away, maybe we should explain—" Bethanny began.

"No, it's all over and done with. Let us all start fresh, shall we?" Carlotta put on her bravest smile as she reached for her napkin and placed it in her lap.

Yes, a fresh start for us all.

Throughout the course of dinner Carlotta found her gaze straying to the door. When a footman would enter to take away their soup bowl or lay out another dish, her heart would thump wildly. She was at war with herself, half of her wishing for the duke to appear and gaze at her with those delicious blue eyes, and half of her hoping that he didn't show up at all.

As dinner ended and the duke didn't appear, she decided that regardless, she got her wish. Though relieved, a part of her —traitorous that it was— wanted to see him, to gauge if anything had changed. As much as she tried to silence her heart, part of it hoped that maybe, *maybe* his quick dismissal after their kiss was his way of covering his own emotions, his own response. The kiss was quite spontaneous. It was highly doubtful he had premeditated it; therefore, it was natural to wonder if maybe he was as unsettled as she.

But she wasn't to know, because he wasn't to make an appearance.

"Come girls, let's retire to the library to read for a spell before bed." Carlotta rose and waited for the girls to follow suit. With a slight inclination of her head, she motioned to the door. The three girls filed out and walked quietly down the hall. Bethanny opened the large door for the rest of them then slipped in quietly, holding the latch so that when it shut, it was noiseless.

"You're all very quiet," Carlotta noted, her eyes narrowing with suspicion, then widening with concern. Were they feeling poorly? Were they sick? Perhaps the rain—

"We're simply... tired," Beatrix mumbled, sniffing.

"Oh. Well you are certainly able to retire if you wish," Carlotta responded, carefully watching their expressions, evaluating the color of their skin, and searching for a cause for their strange behavior.

As she watched the girls, she saw a flicker of a glance, one that passed between Bethanny and Beatrix, which caused her to pause. It was just the type of glance she believed she would give in a conspiratorial manner if she had a sister. But she was an only child, so she simply stored away the thought to ponder on later. It wasn't as if they could get into too much trouble.

She quickly amended her last thought. Judging by the fiasco earlier in the duke's study, there was quite a bit of trouble they could find. Maybe she should follow them to bed.

"You know, I'm quite exhausted myself, I'll follow—"

"No!" Beatrix shouted. She was promptly kicked by Bethanny.

"It's just that—er—we don't want to cause you further trouble," Bethanny said softly. After a delicate pause, she took a few steps forward towards Carlotta. "We've caused enough trouble today. We can see to ourselves and you'll surely enjoy a few moments of respite." Bethanny's wide eyes were full of innocent intentions, bottomless and guiltless.

The girl was a skilled liar.

But Carlotta allowed them their deception. If she asked them outright, they'd likely never admit to anything. But if she kept her eye out, she'd easily uncover whatever folly they had planned. She only hoped it didn't involve the duke. Heaven knew, she couldn't deal with another scenario that would require her to speak with him in private.

Her heart would surely crack.

"Well, goodnight then, girls. That is, if you're sure—"

"Very sure." This from Beatrix, who nodded emphatically.

As if she needed further proof of something afoot, Beatrix

needlessly provided it.

Bethanny ushered her sisters out the door, much to the outrage of Berty who was bitterly disappointed she was unable to stay up.

The room was quiet, too quiet. The grandfather clock ticked, the fire crackled and then, there was nothing else but the sound of her breathing. Truly she shouldn't be so disturbed by the lack of noise. At Garden Gate it had often been quiet, especially following the deaths of her parents. With no siblings to run about with, she only had her household staff that cared for her, along with the governess she had dismissed upon reaching eighteen. The governess, who had upon her dismissal, run off to Gretna Green with the neighbor's footman. But, in her defense, he was quite a handsome rogue. For all Carlotta knew, they were in Scotland still. Miss March was pleasant enough, but wasn't one to expend extra energy on her charge. Apparently, she *had* spent her energy on the neighbor's footman, however. While Carlotta wished her well, she felt no resentment at her actions or the distance at which she kept her charge. But that experience was why she felt such a need to build a relationship with Berty, Bethanny and Beatrix.

She'd never had someone do that for her.

And now, she found herself in the position *to* do just that. Regardless of the trouble they caused, either by their mysterious plotting, or inadvertent mishap, they would grow through their tragedy knowing they were loved.

Even if it were just by a governess.

****

Charles paced like a caged animal. At least ten times, he strode to the study door to open it then pulled his hand back as if the doorknob had grown teeth.

Then he'd pace back to his desk, pick up a few papers.

Gaze at them, see absolutely nothing except for her face. After which, he'd march back to the door, only to have the whole bloody scenario repeat again and again.

He never once thought of himself as a coward. However, he was beginning to reevaluate his thoughts. What was it? He was the Duke of Clairmont! His reputation was the stuff of legends! He'd sampled the pleasures of many high profile courtesans and opera singers in the country, some even from *other* countries. He, who easily discouraged the pesky dandy with a simple scowl, was hiding behind his own study door because of a woman.

No, a virgin young lady.

Who wasn't noble. Who was his governess.

Well, not *his* governess, his wards' governess... but that made her under his employ and technically *his* governess as well... it got confusing after that. So he poured himself a glass of brandy, relishing the fiery trail it blazed to his stomach. He drained the glass, and promptly poured himself another.

As he sipped, he tried to think of a way that would let Carlotta know he was, well, what was he exactly? Sorry? No. He damn well wasn't sorry about kissing her. That was quite possibly the most perfect kiss he'd experienced in some time. And he'd just insult her further if he said he was sorry. She'd take it all wrong. Being female, she'd think he regretted *her*. Which he did, but not in the way she thought. Or would think... or...

"What in the bloody hell happened to all the brandy?" he said to no one in particular, because he was alone.

A warm sensation began tingling in his toes, spreading to his other limbs before settling with its center in his belly. As a few minutes passed and he stared into the fire, he began to feel a bit more, able. Able to leave, that is. His study. He glanced about the room. Yes. That's where he was. His stomach rumbled, and he tried to remember when he had last eaten. Noon? No...

"Hang it all." He spoke to the fire. "Bloody governess. Coming in, waltzing in and stealing my... thoughts. Yes! My thoughts. I never was one to be so... unthoughtful," he grumbled. "You know—" Again, he spoke to no one in particular. "—I don't have to apologize! I'm a duke! I bloody well take what I want! I wanted a kiss. I took it. There. That's the end. If I want another kiss, I'll simply... well..." He realized with a wave of annoyance at himself, that though quite deep in his cups at this point, he was not *that* drunk to steal another kiss. Or take another kiss, or whatever had happened. At this point, it was all growing quite fuzzy. Perhaps if he were to eat dinner?

He glanced to the door then remembered he was trapped. Dinner. If he were to go to dinner, he'd see the governess. *Carlotta, Miss Lottie... Miss Carlottie...* He shook his head. Blast and Damn.

He couldn't bloody well starve.

It was his house after all; he had to leave his study sometime. With a fortifying breath and summoning the courage only a blasphemous amount of brandy could incite, he barreled through the door.

"Ah-ha!" He thrust his fist in the air in victory. He glanced back to the door. "You have been bested!" He pointed at the offending portal.

Squaring his shoulders, he pulled his coat up, and smoothed his shirt, tightening his cravat. With purpose and victory brimming his chest, he strode to the dining room... finding it empty. Of both food and people.

"Bloody—"

"Your grace?"

"Murray!" Charles jumped slightly, casting his butler a severely annoyed expression.

"Your grace, are you quite all right?" Murray asked. His tone was monotone but his grey eyes narrowed slightly, as if concerned.

It was possibly the first hint at emotion he'd ever seen from his butler.

And enough to cause him to lose his train of thought.

Perhaps that was simply the brandy, however.

"Your grace... are you... well?" Murray drew out the words, his lean body leaning forward as he studied Charles.

"Of course. I was just wondering when we planned on dining."

"Your grace, my sincerest apologies... dinner was served quite a while ago. Mrs. Pott searched for you, but when she was unable to locate you, assumed you had gone out, your grace." Murray nodded nervously.

Charles glanced down to the polished floor. He did have a faint memory of Mrs. Pott knocking on his study door. Why had he not said anything?

Ah yes, the governess. He was hiding.

No, not *hiding.*

He was thinking. Yes. That sounded ever so much better than hiding.

Which he wasn't.

"Your grace?"

Murray probably thought he'd lost all his sense. "Yes, well... please have Cook send a tray to my chamber."

"Of course, your grace." Murray bowed and departed to the kitchens.

Charles strode out into the hall. "That worked well," he mumbled to himself.

"What worked well, your grace?"

"Ack! Berta, Roberty. Whatever your name is!" He calmed his racing heart and adjusted his coat, trying to at least appear in control of himself.

"Berty. My name is Berty," the little girl said a wry tone.

"Where... no... what are you doing?" Charles' nerves were already shot, if one more person startled him, he couldn't be held responsible for his actions.

The little girl shrugged.

"Where are your sisters?" Charles asked, glancing up and down the hall quickly.

"In their room." She leaned forward. "They're... wait. I can't tell *you*." She gasped and covered her mouth.

"Tell me what...?" Charles leaned down to Berty's eye level.

"Well if I told *you* then it would be a disaster. You'd ruin it!"

"I'd ruin it? How so?" Curiosity mixed with severe apprehension clenched in his chest.

"Because well... it just would."

"Your logic is indisputable." Charles spoke tiredly.

"Thank you, your grace." Berty curtsied.

Was she mocking him?

She batted her dark eyelashes.

She *was* mocking him!

"Now see here Berty—"

"Berty! What are you still doing up?" Carlotta's voice floated down the hall.

Charles found himself swallowing hard. *So much for avoidance.* As she walked towards them, he found himself lifting his gaze to watch her approach. She had changed from her wet gown into a deep green dress that showed off the curve of her hips and the smallest swell of her breasts. Her eyes were fixed on Berty but he could swear he saw the faintest hint of a blush deepen the pinkish hue of her cheeks.

She was delicious.

"Berty?" she asked again.

"They were too loud!" Berty wined.

"Pardon?"

"They were whispering, loudly. And every time I asked a question, they'd tell me to hush. So I left."

"Understandable," Charles commented.

Carlotta raised an eyebrow.

"I'm simply stating that if someone told *me* to hush, I'd have left too."

"I highly doubt you'd simply *leave* if someone spoke to you that way."

"Perhaps you're right…" Charles felt his lips twitch into a smile.

Carlotta regarded him for a moment before turning her attention to Berty. "Love, you need to return to your room. Remember what we spoke about this afternoon?"

"But Miss Lottie! I'm in the hall. The *hallway!* I *am* obeying you! Ask his grace! I was not being disruptive."

"Any one." Carlotta spoke the words at the same time as he did. He glanced to her, their eyes meeting.

"Any*one*." Berty sighed, correcting herself… and breaking the spell.

"Be that as it may… you still should head to your room. It's quite late and you've had a busy day."

Charles cleared his throat.

Carlotta glanced at him, her eyes unreadable but he could have sworn he saw mirth dancing in their green depths.

"Very well," Berty conceded, shrugging and then skipping down the hall.

Charles watched her leave and as she ducked around the corner, he reluctantly glanced back to Carlotta.

She was still watching where Berty had gone.

So he waited, studying her profile, memorizing the way her pert nose turned up slightly, and the way her jawline angled into the most delicate bow just below her ear. He wanted to kiss her in that precise spot.

"You can't avoid me forever." Charles spoke in a low and seductive whisper. Wincing inwardly at how the words should be aimed at him.

"I'm not avoiding you." She gave him a sidelong glance.

"Oh?"

"No, I was… wondering."

"About what? Or whom, perhaps?"

"Do you have siblings, your grace?" Carlotta turned the full power of her gaze to him. It was stunning. Her green eyes had flicks of yellow in them that almost appeared gold.

"Your grace?"

"No. No siblings. Not for want of trying on my parents' part, however," he added, though as he spoke the words he wondered why he had thought that information was important.

"Oh. Nor do I..." Her gaze traveled back down the hall where Berty had disappeared.

"You suspect something," he stated.

"Yes. But I haven't a clue as to what. Which, I'll admit, makes me slightly nervous."

"There are three of them." Charles nodded. "And all quite intelligent. I shudder to think what they might be planning."

"You and I both. I'll have to keep a keen eye on them."

"As opposed to?" Charles couldn't help but grin.

"As opposed to giving them any chance to... interfere with the lives of others."

"Sounds utterly wise."

"I rather thought you'd agree." She turned back, flashing a saucy grin. But as soon as the alluring expression crossed her features, she withdrew it, shuttering her expression into a polite mask.

Charles wanted the saucy expression back. He wanted to see the merriment dancing in her eyes, hear the dry whit of her humor and see the way her cheeks squinted her eyes slightly when she smiled.

"Carlotta, I..." he began, not quite sure what he had intended to say.

"There's no need, your grace." She offered him a damnably polite smile that didn't reach her eyes and quickly glanced down at the polished floor.

Charles opened his mouth, intending to say... something but words failed him. He rather wanted to *show* her what he meant, but knew that would be disaster. He could not kiss her again.

Ever.

Ever, ever, ever.

But oh, he wanted to.

He was sure that a kiss to that delicate spot he was lusting over earlier would surely break through the miserably shuttered expression in her eyes. He was sure that he could coax more than a polite 'your grace' from her lips. At once he wanted to hear her voice whisper his name. Not 'Clairmont', not 'your grace', but his actual name. *Charles.*

She lifted her gaze, her eyes slowly trailing her movement till they met his. With a small gasp, her eyes widened and she stepped back.

"Good evening, your grace." She curtsied and all but fled.

As her footsteps echoed in the hall, he felt cold and empty. As if the fire he was standing in front of had suddenly been smothered. The emptiness was gnawing at him. He felt like a coward for not saying anything about their kiss, but he didn't know how to go about it. If she were more than a servant, more than a governess, there might have been a chance.

But she wasn't.

And he wasn't the type of man to marry, at least yet. Or so he reminded himself. Strange how he always forgot that piece of information whenever she was around.

Closing his eyes he remembered her expression just before she fled to the safety of her room. She'd had the wide-eyed expression of a woman running from ruin, from certain danger.

Which meant *he* was the threat, the danger.

That thought didn't set well with him at all. It also meant that she had quite accurately read his thoughts, though they likely had been quite apparent in his expression. An innocent wouldn't know how to discern between lust and desire. Few knew that there even was a difference.

Lust was shallower, fleeting and purely selfish; a burn that flashed rather than smoldered. Whereas desire, it was a slower burn that tended to flare up at times, but never truly burn out. Desire required one to think about the other person, it involved restraint for selfless reasons. Desire scorched.

What he felt for Carlotta may have initially been lust.

But he was definitely feeling singed at the moment.

His stomach ached.

He needed to get her out of his house. He needed to distance himself, and her, from the temptation. Tomorrow. The rain had slowed and stopped shortly after their return from the park. If it stayed away overnight, the roads might at least be passable. If so, then he'd see that she and the girls left for his estate in Bath on the morrow. It was the only way. With distance, his body would cool and he'd once again be able to *think*. Rather than simply act.

He strode towards his chambers with renewed purpose. But with each step, he felt emptiness like a cavern grow within him.

Of course, that could simply be because he *was* hungry.

He just didn't want to think about for what…

****

"Miss Carlotta?" Mrs. Pott pulled Carlotta's attention away from the packed trunk beside her bed and towards the door.

"Yes?" she responded. All morning her presence of mind had been unforgivably absent. When she learned that they were to depart to Bath that morning, conflicting emotions had slammed into her chest, warring for dominance.

They continued to battle.

On one hand, Carlotta felt relived. It would be infinitely easier to take care of the girls, to teach and tutor them without the dark and delicious presence of the duke. She knew that if they stayed, she'd always be distracted, wondering if he were to pass by, or speak to her.

The girls deserved better than that.

Yet, at the same time, her heart stung with the bite of rejection. The venom of insecurity swirled around her mind. *Why* was he having them leave, and on such short notice? She knew he was intending on moving the girls to the estate in Bath, but as he came to know them, she rather hoped he'd want to be more of a part of their lives.

And maybe of her life too.

But even as her mind whispered the words to her heart, she bit back a sarcastic laugh. She must be delusional to even entertain the slightest thought of the duke paying her mind. While he did kiss her —and oh, what a kiss it had been!— she wasn't foolish enough to entertain serious thoughts about his intentions. It would only invite heartbreak.

Her father's words echoed in her mind. "The *quality* do not fraternize with those who are not. It's simply not done."

She relived that particular lecture after her father discovered her frolicking with the stable master's son, Rory. It had been innocent enough. Rory was a few years her senior, and had been a friend since she was quite young. She had been but twelve, that blessedly awkward stage where she was no longer a child yet, not yet a woman. Rory had invited her to skip rocks and she quickly agreed. They had their usual competitive banter, but then something changed. In hindsight, she realized that Rory was about more than simply skipping rocks, but at the time, she simply noticed how his hand felt warm on hers when he tried to show her a new way to skip the rock. He had whispered the instructions in her ear, in a low tone that had made her skin erupt in goose bumps.

She'd followed his instructions and skipped the rock.

Upon turning her head she had realized just how close he was, and how he smelled like leather and cedar.

Her father called her name not a moment later.

As her father beckoned her to attend him to the house, she didn't miss the piercing gaze he shot to Rory. Once inside, Father had led her to library.

"Dear Lottie," he began and proceeded to explain the difference between those titled and those not. It was a lengthy lecture, running all together in her memory, but one part seemed *too* clear, hauntingly so. It mocked her now.

"Those who are titled never, ever fraternize with the servants."

Never ever.

Of course, her father could have never foreseen that the daughter he delighted in would one day be forced into the position of governess. No season, no marriage mart, no advantageous match, and no further titled generations roaming the halls of Garden Gate. All of that disappeared when the money was lost. Granted, she still was the daughter of a baron; impoverished as she was, however, she might as well be the daughter of a merchant for all the good her father's title did for her now.

"Carlotta?" Mrs. Pott called again.

Pulled from her musings, she turned to the housekeeper who had just let herself in.

"Forgive me, but when you didn't respond, I thought perhaps you were finished and had already left to see the girls.

"I was woolgathering I'm afraid."

"No need to apologize." Mrs. Pott gave her a warm and maternal smile. "Are you almost finished?"

"Yes, I don't have terribly much to pack. In fact..." Carlotta stood and smoothed her skirt. "I believe I'm finished."

"Wonderful. I'll have a footman come and take your trunk to the carriage. You'll love Greenford Waters, near Bath,

Miss Lottie. It's truly a dream. The gardens are my favorite part. I've only been once, attending the late Dowager, but I'll not forget it."

"I'm sure it will be beautiful."

Carlotta felt a slight pain of loss as well as anticipation. After all, Bath was quite close to Garden Gate. Perhaps she could find out just how the estate was managing without her. Mr. Burrows had taken care of all the particulars so she had all faith that all was as well as could be expected, however, it would be wonderful to see it for herself.

"I'll go and check on the girls." Carlotta nodded to Mrs. Pott and entered the hall. The gilded artwork and opulent furnishings of the duke's London residence were beautiful, but she hoped that the estate in Bath was a little less, intimidating. All one had to do was simply meet the duke to realize the power and wealth he possessed, the house was simply an overstatement. Not overdone, but a reminder that was unnecessary. Though she supposed it was probably common among the *ton*.

"Beatrix! I promise it will all work out simply beautifully. You'll see. I have all faith—"

"All faith in what?" Carlotta asked as she pushed open the already ajar door into the girls' room.

"Uh…" Bethanny stammered, her eyes widening and glancing to Beatrix, who simply shook her head and took a step back.

"Oh, Miss Lottie! I'm so very excited! I hope the duke's house has gardens so we can run and play tag. Maybe there's even a pond! Do you think?" Berty had rushed up to Carlotta and grabbed her hands, jumping in place while she squeezed her fingers tightly.

"I'm sure there will be plenty of garden for you to roam about and frolic, little one." Carlotta bent down and tugged teasingly on Berty's plait.

"I knew it." She sighed happily.

"Are you three about ready? The sooner we leave the sooner we'll get there." Carlotta glanced at the older two.

"Of course. Do… that is… is his grace expected to send us off?" Bethanny asked bashfully.

"I'm not sure." Carlotta bit her lip nervously. One would *expect* that he would indeed, see them off. But she wondered.

"Mrs. Pott already said goodbye," Beatrix commented as she put on her bonnet.

"Did she?"

"Yes! And I think Mr. Murray will miss us. He seemed terribly sad," Berty commented.

"Murray?" Carlotta couldn't help the wry and disbelieving tone her words carried. Not once had she even seen the butler carry an expression that varied from polite distance.

"Oh yes! He's quite kind, you know. Always sneaking us sweets."

Carlotta raised her eyebrows in disbelief. "And when did he do this?"

"Oh, well here and there. You usually weren't around. I don't think he wanted to be caught."

Carlotta looked to Bethanny and Beatrix, who had small grins teasing their lips. "I had no idea."

"He really is a dear man. He has a few granddaughters our age."

"I believe you know more about him than even the duke does."

"I suspect so. We will miss him, and Mrs. Pott. They have been so lovely." Bethanny said.

"Indeed." Carlotta nodded absentmindedly. She was still trying to wrap her head around the idea of Murray sneaking about the house to slip the girl's sweets. Truly, wonders never cease.

"I'll let Mrs. Pott know we're all set. Don't forget your bonnet, Berty."

Berty shot her a mutinous glare and picked up her bonnet as if an unsavory insect.

Carlotta waited patiently.

Berty narrowed her eyes, huffed indignantly, and then proceeded to tie it under her chin.

Very slowly.

Carlotta nodded and left. Murray was waiting in the foyer. Carlotta held back, studying the butler with new eyes. Tilting her head, she tried to imagine him hiding peppermints or something else in his pockets.

"Care to tell me what we are spying on? Or whom?" a rich baritone asked from just behind her.

Carlotta jumped, her hand instinctively flying to her heart. "Your grace! You gave me a fright!"

"Forgive me, you were quite intent on your study of Murray. I'm greatly curious as to the reason." His eyes danced with merriment and a far too alluring light of mischief.

"It would seem your butler leads a secret life." Carlotta raised her eyebrow dramatically.

"You have my complete attention, Miss Lottie." He inclined his head towards her, a wicked gleam in his eye.

"Though as I consider it, perhaps I shouldn't tell you. I wouldn't want to break a confidence."

"Dear Miss Lottie. I can assure you that anything you were about to disclose is likely already known by me. Murray is entirely predictable." He shrugged his broad shoulders.

Carlotta tried to not to notice how his jacket accented just how broad they were. So she pried her gaze from his jacket to his eyes.

Which was a mistake. They were warm, inviting, and harboring a delightful twinkle. It was a deadly combination, so she glanced to his lips, which reminded her of their kiss. Was there anywhere she could focus her attention that wouldn't cause her mind to freeze up like a shallow puddle in January?

Desperately trying to gather her wits, she blurted,

"Murray sneaks the girls sweets."

She glanced down to the floor. Clearly, it was the only safe place to rest her gaze, everywhere else simply was too much.

****

"Pardon?" Charles felt his jaw drop. When Carlotta said his butler led a secret life, he was anticipating… well he wasn't sure what but it was *not* that he was smuggling sweets to the girls.

In fact, he didn't remember ever seeing Murray around the girls.

"Are you quite sure?" Charles asked, his tone disbelieving.

"I had the same response," Carlotta replied with a wry grin. Her berry red lips were twisted up to one side and her green eyes danced with delight.

"I say… I didn't think he had it in him." Charles shook his head then turned his attention to his old butler once more, studying him in a new light.

"Yes. Bethanny said that they reminded him of his granddaughters."

"Murray has a family?"

"It would appear so."

"Oh, I suppose I never really thought about it."

"Apparently," Carlotta murmured. Charles rather thought he wasn't intended to hear, so he pretended that he did not.

Just like he pretended not to smile.

Charles watched Carlotta as she tilted her head, studying Murray. Her neck was graceful and slender. Her body radiated warmth that wasn't felt as much as sensed. It warmed his soul. Her lips drew his attention once more as he tipped into a small smile, one of innocent amusement.

It had been a long time since he saw a smile like that.

Oh, he had seen plenty of smiles. Too many. Most of them directed towards him with some degree of selfish intent. But a smile that was innocently taking joy without requiring anything in return… *that* was as rare as hen's teeth. Especially in the *ton*.

So he stared at her, memorizing the way her cheeks curved causing her eyes to squint slightly. Like a refreshing breeze in the stifling heat of summer, he let her fresh innocence wash over him.

Until she turned.

Clearing his throat, he tried to appear as if he weren't caught staring.

Which he most certainly was.

But being a duke did have its advantages. If he didn't speak of it, then *most* people would pretend it never happened.

"Why were you staring?"

Of course, *most* people didn't include her. No, that would have been to bloody lucky.

And apparently, all luck had flown out the window once she had arrived.

"I was… taking delight in how my butler clearly amused you." He spoke smoothly, praying urgently that she'd not question his answer.

Her eyes narrowed slightly, but she nodded. "We are all ready to depart, your grace. The girls… they were wondering if you were going to see them off?"

"The girls?" he asked, searching her eyes intently for a hint of whether she was wishing for his presence as well.

"Well yes…" Her brow furrowed as she met his gaze.

And because he couldn't help but ask, "*Just* the girls?" He leaned in, closing the distance and inhaling the alluring scent of apricots and fresh laundry.

"I—I—" she stammered. Her eyes widened, her sooty

lashes brushing her winged brows as she struggled to answer his forward question.

He shouldn't have glanced to her lips. It was a miserable idea. Come to think of it, he didn't actually *think* about glancing there, but was drawn outside of his own will. He *needed* to see them. To commit them to memory. She was leaving.

Of course, she was leaving at his behest; however, that didn't mean he didn't wish the circumstances were different.

Why couldn't she have been an impoverished earl's daughter?

Her lips parted as she took in a deeper breath.

This time Charles took a split second to think, to consider exactly what he was doing even as he proceeded to close the distance between their lips. He could have backed away, he could have quipped something witty with his devil may care attitude.

But he didn't.

Damning his own weakness, he admitted that he was indeed powerless against her.

And as his lips brushed hers, he thought that maybe, being powerful was overrated.

She stiffened as his lips caressed hers, causing him to hesitate before deepening the kiss. His body demanded more, aching for more but he held himself firmly in check.

Of course, *now* his self-control decided to make an appearance.

He teased her lower lip with his tongue, inhaling deeply so that the full effect; her scent, her taste, the slight sound of her breathing all added to the symphony of her kiss.

He'd never heard more beautiful music.

She relaxed slightly, just enough to encourage him and he pressed his lips slightly firmer against hers, increasing the pressure and sliding his tongue along the seam of her lips. She trembled, but didn't back away. His hands moved to her shoulders, resting on them and memorizing the texture of her dress, the shape of her arms as his hands traveled down to her fingers, where he held onto her dainty glove-covered hands.

He couldn't remember the last time he held a woman's hand for the simple pleasure of just touching her. It was blissful and remarkably intimate. Though he desperately wanted to remove her gloves and feel the heat of her skin on his.

As if remembering herself, she backed away abruptly, breaking their exchange. Her eyes were wide and glossy, as if restraining tears.

Charles felt his own chest constricting as he realized he was the cause.

"Your grace, I—"

"Car—Miss Lottie, please. Don't." He held up his hand and took a deep breath.

She nodded, her posture full of bravado, and Charles swore he saw her building a wall around herself, as if she needed extra armor to protect against him.

If he hadn't already felt like a cad, that would have pushed him over the edge.

"Miss Lottie." His chest ached at the words he knew he must say. His body warred against itself, knowing the truth but wanting desperately to find a way to make it not matter.

But some things just couldn't be changed.

"I find that moving you and the girls to my estate in Bath is the wisest choice for us both. I'll freely admit that my attraction to you is unacceptable and therefore, I'm removing you from my presence and quite honestly, from temptation. I'll see that every need you and the girls have is immediately met and please, if you do need anything, do not hesitate to ask Tibbs. He's the butler at Greenford Waters. Please give my regards to the girls, I don't... think it prudent that I see them off myself." He bowed and left.

The horrifically accepting and humble expression in her

eyes haunted his memory as he walked away, mocking him.

****

"I still don't understand why his grace didn't say good bye," Berty pouted in the corner of the carriage as they made their way to the countryside.

"He told me to give you his regards." Carlotta spoke over the thick lump in her throat. Even after riding in the carriage for several hours, she still felt like at any moment she might dissolve into tears.

"But it's particularly *rude* to not say goodbye," Berty complained.

"Berty, hush," Bethanny scolded, her eyes traveling to Carlotta and then darting away.

Obviously she was piecing things together. Which was exactly what Carlotta *didn't* want.

"How long till we reach Bath?" Beatrix asked quietly.

"It's about a day and half trip. His grace has made arrangements for us to stay at an inn in Oxfordshire. We'll stay there tonight, wake early and travel a little over half a day to Bath." Carlotta used her all her inner strength to pull herself together. These girls needed her; she'd not fail them over some weak and futile heartbreak.

It wasn't as if she didn't know better. She *did* know better, but that didn't prevent it from hurting. She *knew* it was futile to further the overwhelming attraction that ignited between them whenever it pleased, but hearing it from *his* lips… it was a wretched dose of reality and still stung.

She never thought he'd break the rules of society and pursue *her*. She had more common sense than that, but she would have liked for him too. As futile as it was, she just couldn't seem to communicate that information to her traitorous heart.

Her throat constricted as she remembered his words, but

his expression spoke volumes more. His dancing blue eyes were cold, polite and distant, his words clipped and cool, and his posture ridged. Everything he said seemed at odds with his body language. And quite honestly, she didn't know which to believe. His words were kind, gentle even as he was more honest than was necessary, but it didn't remove the sting from the implications.

He wanted her gone.

For her good, but also for his. She couldn't hold that against him. But it didn't sit well, being so easily disregarded. Her first taste of romance and she had to go and find the most unattainable bachelor in the country.

It miserably aligned with the rest of her recent luck.

But she refused to dwell on it. As she glanced over to the girls, she resolved to leave it behind like the dust from London. Like the smoky and foul heavy air, she'd dismiss it and embrace the fresh air of the future. Who knew? Maybe this temporary heartbreak —because it *was* temporary, she'd see that it was!— would make her stronger, wiser. And maybe she'd fall in love with someone kind, fiercely attractive and *available* in Bath.

And she couldn't forget Garden Gate. Being in Bath would be, in a way, like being home. She'd visited the city often as a child and with her home so close, she could hopefully see it.

The day was looking brighter all the time.

Beatrix was staring out the window, Bethanny was reading, and Berty had promptly fallen asleep and was leaning against Carlotta's shoulder. Her heart might be bruised, but she'd make sure it wasn't broken. And above all, she wasn't alone.

Chapter Six

Charles tried not to watch the carriage pull away, but he couldn't seem to pry his gaze away from the Blood Bays as they clipped down the street and out of sight.

He was doing the right thing.

Or so he tried to remind himself. He was being noble, honorable even, in sending her way.

Damn it all.

Of course, the time he decided to be honorable was with the only woman he could never have, the only woman he ever wanted so badly and the only woman he should probably never see again.

Life was never this complicated before. He closed his eyes, remembering her face, her scent, and the wide-eyed expression of wonder after the first time he kissed her.

She was gone. He sent her away. Could the day get any worse?

"Your grace? You have a caller? Lady Southridge," Murray said.

Apparently, it can get worse.

"Ah yes. I've been expecting her. Show her in to the

green salon, I'll be there shortly."

"Very good your grace." Murray bowed and left.

"Blast it all, Graham. You owe me," he muttered under his breath as he left his study and walked down the hall towards the green salon. *Better to get this over and through with.*

"Lady Southridge! What a delight to see you!" Charles gave her his most charming grin.

"Your grace," she responded, her eyes studying him in the most disconcerting manner. Charles always felt as if she saw through him, examining his very thoughts.

Heaven forbid.

Lady Southridge was one of the few people who wasn't intimidated by him. She sat demurely on the settee, her posture perfect, her hair immaculate and her clothes impeccably fashionable. Few knew the iron will beneath the silk. But he did, and he was trying very hard not to be nervous.

Though Graham was several years younger than he, they had become fast friends, which led them into a few scrapes. All of which Lady Southridge had known about, lectured them over and promptly executed judgment. Charles' parents weren't alive to do so, so she took the role upon herself. She was really quite a maternal figure in Charles' life as well, much as he reluctantly admitted. Which was why he was so apprehensive. For all intents and purposes, he felt like he was the brother taking the fall for the younger sibling.

"I'll not keep you. I'm assuming you've been delegated to tell me of my brother's recent retreat to Scotland?" She spoke with a bored tone.

"Why, yes. Did Graham tell you himself then?"

She gave him a withering glare that seemed to say, *you can't be serious.*

"My brother wouldn't tell me if he were leaving for China. That's why I have to find out these things for myself, you know. By the way, how are your wards?"

"My wards? But—"

"I have my ways. Don't worry your secret is safe. Lord knows how many secrets I'm keeping safe for you. I'll simply add this one to the list." She held up a gloved hand and seemed to study the leather, her brow creasing for a moment. She turned her gaze to him, a lack of patience quite clear in her expression.

"Well, they are in Bath, or on their way at the moment," Charles said. After answering, he had the overwhelming urge to loosen his cravat.

"Bath? Why did you send them away? Hoydens are they?"

"No, not particularly at least. They are actually quite… nice…"

"Don't choke on it, your grace." She raised a delicate eyebrow.

"You can quit with the 'your grace's' Lady Southridge." Charles grew irritated.

She grinned. "Of course, *Charles*. But why? Why move them to Bath? Surely, the city has more diversion for them? What are their ages?"

"Bethanny is sixteen, Beatrix is twelve, and Berty is seven."

"The oldest will need a season soon," she remarked.

"Indeed."

"I must object to your sending them away. As a young lady about to make her debut, she must be in London to learn some of the more intricate social graces. Of course her governess… you *did* hire a governess for the girls." She narrowed her eyes. "And please tell me you were wiser than I'm anticipating and you hired an old woman." She closed her eyes as if in silent prayer.

"Of course I hired a governess! I'm not daft! What do you think?" Charles shook his head and stomped to the fire, purposefully not answering her second question. Something about being in the presence of someone parental brought out the inner child of even a duke.

"Good. What's her name?"

"Who?" Charles asked stubbornly. He didn't want to think about her, not around Lady Southridge. She'd smell the smoke from the smoldering heat of desire still swirling within him.

"The governess." She drew it out, likely thinking him daft.

Better daft than emotionally involved.

"Miss Carlotta Standhope."

"Standhope? Any relation to the Standhopes of Garden Gate?" Lady Southridge's tone was curious. "I thought Sinclair had a daughter named something similar. But I think they called her Lottie. I can't be sure. Was quite a while ago. They both died you know. I wonder what happened to the girl. Hmm, she would be quite young." She seemed to be lost in her own thoughts and Charles was happy to let her wander there however long she wanted.

Whatever it took to keep the attention off him and the blasted governess. Though he did sense an underlying reason for her question.

"Charles?" she asked after a moment.

"I'm not sure who her relations are. I've only had her acquaintance for a short time." But not nearly long enough, yet at the same time, far too long. A price he was paying for dearly.

"Ah."

Charles refused to rise to her bait. She was only quiet for one reason; hoping someone would fill the silence and say more than they intended.

He'd fallen for that trap too many times, trying to fill the silence with an overplay of the story that was certainly fabricated in order to alleviate himself or Graham from responsibility or punishment. Usually both. Graham had learned the same lesson.

"You're awfully quiet." Lady Southridge commented, her eyes narrowing while she studied him.

"Not much to say," Charles said, rocking on his heels.

"So when will you see the girls again?" Lady Southridge asked after a moment.

"I'm not quite sure. I hadn't planned on seeing them at all, actually."

"Charles! I'm disappointed in you! Surely, you were planning on seeing them shortly! These girls have no one save a *governess* and you're their only family."

"I'm sure Miss Lottie will take good care of them."

"A governess is not a replacement for a guardian," she shot back.

"Carlotta is perfectly able to—"

"Carlotta is it? My, my your quite familiar with that old crone of a governess." Lady Southridge's tone was overly pleased, like a cat sipping cream.

"She's not an old crone! *Miss* Carlotta came on highest praise and the girls adore her. It's simple as that." Charles continued to watch the fire, unwilling to turn around lest Lady Southridge read his emotions all too clearly.

Of course, that didn't stop her from rising and coming to stand beside him.

Bloody Hell.

"I think…" she began as she studied his face, "that next week we should go and visit your wards."

"Excuse me?" Charles felt his eyes grow wide from both fear and hope. Fear because Lady Southridge used the word *we,* and anticipation because more than anything he wanted to see Carlotta. Just see her.

Not kiss her.

See. Her. Only.

"Yes. I think it's a brilliant idea."

"You would," Charles muttered.

"I heard that," Lady Southridge whispered.

"Of course you did. What about Lord Southridge? He'd not want you—"

"Pish and tosh! Of course he wouldn't mind! He's visiting Bristol that week anyway, I'd be closer to him in Bath than if I were to stay in London."

"But—"

"You're not going to get out of this Charles. Neither you nor Graham seem inclined to get married and produce an heir, therefore you both must be blamed for causing me to resort to adopting your wards. They'll need a sponsor once they debut and I'm the best they can get. Lord knows I've earned the right to spoil three girls after putting up with you and Graham all these years. You honestly seek to deny me that?" She speared him with a daring gaze.

"No." Because what else could he say?

"Delightful! I'll make arrangements to leave for Bath in a week's time." She nodded and strode to the door.

"Of course," Charles responded tightly as he bowed.

"And Charles?"

"Yes?"

"Please attend me in three days' time at the Worthing ball. Lord Southridge is unable to attend and I need an escort."

"A delight, my lady." He responded with a clenched jaw, trying to be cordial when all he wanted was for the blasted woman to leave.

"Of course it is." Her delicate eyebrow lifted in mirth as her hazel eyes danced.

She let herself out of the study, and Charles collapsed on a nearby chair, puffing out a great sigh. Lady Southridge was a force not to be reckoned with. Graham owed him. Owed him well.

But he couldn't deny a swell of joy and anticipation in the prospect of seeing Carlotta in a week's time. He tried to tell himself that he wouldn't count the days... but he knew he would.

Now if he could only think of a way to get out of attending the Worthing ball.

****

Charles studied the whirling dancers in the middle of the ballroom at the Worthing ball three days later. He swirled the warm champagne in his glass and tried to not appear as bored as he was. He had already danced with Lady Worth then retreated to one of the gaming rooms. That had proved tedious after a while, so he went to the edge of the ballroom and watched.

The debutantes were all in a pale green that seemed to be all the rage this season. He studiously avoided the corner where the dowagers and matchmaking mommas were in conspiracy against his fellow men. There was no way he'd walk into that dragon's lair, but that didn't stop them from sending him calculating glances or their daughters from parading in front of him on the way to the refreshment table.

Never mind the refreshment table was on the other side of the ballroom.

"Your grace." A velvety voice spoke just to his left. Without turning, he knew to whom the voice belonged. Lady Beckham was a merry widow who was known for her expensive taste and perusal of men.

"Lady Beckham. How are you this evening?" Charles spoke in his most seductive tone simply out of habit. He wasn't looking for company that night, but that was a recent occurrence. His taste for the superficial had ended when he got a sampling of something much richer.

Of course, he had sent that temptation away to Bath... but that didn't change the tone of his appetite.

"I'm doing marvelous. What a crush," she said making light conversation.

"Indeed." Charles acknowledged the truth. Indeed, it was a crush. People were lined up against every wall; the ballroom was filled as well as all the gaming rooms. Lord and Lady Worth would be the source of all tomorrow's gossip.

"You seemed so lonely over in this corner. I thought I'd cheer you up. Of course, I can do far more for you if you'd care to escort me somewhere more… private." Her tone was laced with seduction and, a few weeks ago, Charles would have swept her off her feet and found the nearest balcony then taken his fill.

But that was before.

And right now, the last thing he wanted was a cheap imitation of what he knew to be real.

And completely unattainable.

"You do me a great compliment, Lady Beckham. But alas, I must stay close to Lady Southridge as I am her escort tonight."

"Surely she won't miss you for a moment or two," she whispered.

"I'll not risk her ire, my lady. Now, if you'll excuse me." He nodded to her and took his leave, skirting the ballroom till he found Lady Southridge.

"Surviving the crush?" he asked, lowly next to her ear.

She turned and thumped him with her fan. "Don't be impertinent. And never sneak up on a lady," she scolded, but her eyes held a merry twinkle.

"Forgive my manners."

She huffed. "That would imply you had them to begin with."

"You wound me."

"I do not. Lying is a sin, Charles."

"I'm told I've committed a great many." He nodded innocently.

"Save your flirting for your governess," she retorted, her eyebrow rising slightly in challenge.

"What—"

"Don't play with me, and don't panic, for goodness sakes. I didn't say it loud enough for anyone to hear. What do you take me for? Honestly, Charles. Relax."

"I think it's to time leave."

"Scared?"

"Yes. Though you're the only person I'd ever admit that too. And if you ever told a soul I'd deny it."

"I saw Sara trying to hook you."

"Lady Beckham? Yes well… she did not succeed."

"I'm proud of you." She nodded sagely.

"Why, Lady Southridge, I do believe that's a first." Charles grinned teasingly.

"Don't ruin it."

"And our sentimental moment is over."

"Why don't you make yourself useful and order the carriage be brought about. I'm quite weary and wish to depart. One can only survive so many assaults on their intelligence when so many others are found severely lacking."

"Your wish, my command."

Charles left to notify the footman. In short order, they were heading off into the lamplight of Mayfair.

Yet all Charles could think of was how much longer he had to wait until they left for Bath.

****

Greenford Waters, the Duke of Clairmont's estate in Bath, was beautiful and everything that Mrs. Pott promised. The gardens extended for miles, and past them was a wood complete with several fishing ponds and creeks. The girls could wander for days and not reach the end of the property. And the house, rather castle, was breathtaking. The large stone building had several wings that held a myriad of rooms and multiple ballrooms as well. There was a complete Nursery for the girls with a separate schoolroom that had a piano in the corner. Each girl had their own private chambers, but Carlotta noted that they usually spent the night all together, rotating rooms each night.

Life settled into a routine and Carlotta began to feel more like herself. They girls were disappointed that his grace hadn't tried to contact them, or inquire about their welfare. Carlotta tried to her best to allay their disappointment by reminding them just how important and busy their guardian was. In truth, she shouldered the blame herself, more than she cared to admit. After all, he admitted to sending them all away because of her. Did that imply that if she *weren't* the girls' governess that they would have been able to stay with the duke?

Yet as she looked through the leaded glass window at the back gardens, she found comfort in the truth that the girls were far better off in the country than in the stifling city. Originally from Norfolk, the girls had been begging to see the city of Bath, one of the largest in the country.

"Good morning, girls." Carlotta spoke pleasantly to the young ladies as they sat to break their fast.

"Good morning," they murmured collectively. Berty was stifling a yawn and Beatrix was gazing longingly out the window.

"It's quite a lovely day, is it not? Carlotta commented lightly as she buttered a square of toast.

"Indeed." Bethanny smiled sweetly.

"Since it looks as if it might *not* rain… would you girls like to head to town today?"

Three gasps met her ears. "Truly? Truly Miss Lottie?" Berty bounced in her seat, all traces of her lethargy gone.

"Yes. It's a fine day and you've been very patient to wait till we were settled in."

"Can we see The Crescent? And the baths?" Beatrix asked.

"I don't see why not."

"Can we perhaps shop?" Bethanny inquired.

"And have a picnic?" Berty asked, her voice a high pitch in her excitement.

"We shall see. I'll give you an hour after breakfast to ready yourselves. Wear sturdy shoes. While we will be given the convenience of his grace's carriage, we will also be walking quite a bit."

"Yes, Miss Lottie." The girls nodded.

Breakfast was finished in record time and soon they were making their way to the city.

The air was thick with moisture and heavily scented with salt. They crossed the Avon River and clipped their way into the bustling city.

"Where are we to go first?" Bethanny asked excitedly.

"I asked the coachman to drive us around a bit. There's a few places I'd like to show you. Just because were taking a break from your usual studies, doesn't mean we're skipping our lessons entirely."

The girls groaned but it was halfhearted, they were far too delighted to take in all the sights.

As for Carlotta, her heart pinched yet soared at seeing someplace so familiar. Bath was the closest and largest city to Garden Gate. She couldn't count the times she visited. There were a few shops she'd have to avoid for risk of being recognized, as far as beyond that, she was quite certain she would blend in.

"Girls, look to your right. That is the Abby. It was once a Norman church that was built up on a pre-existing foundation. As you can see, most of the buildings are a golden brown color. That's the bath stone, quarried locally. You'll also see your fair share of limestone." Carlotta spoke in her best governess voice, watching her charges eyes widen as they studied the flying buttresses and piercing parapets of the golden colored Abby.

"It's quite fascinating," Beatrix stated. "History and architecture is far more interesting when you can actually *see* it."

"Yes," Berty agreed. "Now where are we going?"

"Next, we'll go through the Circus. Its design was inspired by the Roman Colosseum, but differs in one unique way. While the Colosseum was intended to be seen from the outside, the Circus was intended to be viewed from the inside. It's built in a circular shape with three entrances. Upon entering, you'll notice that the façade of the building is exactly the same no matter where you look."

"How do you know so much about this, Miss Lottie?" Berty asked, her nose scrunched up as she asked.

"I grew up not too far from here," Carlotta answered honestly. She had no need to hide that information from the girls.

"You did? Where?"

"Perhaps I'll take you there to visit sometime, but not today. Now, let's talk about the Crescent."

Carlotta spoke about all the different buildings, their stone and history, until they came to Sydney Park.

"How beautiful!" Berty exclaimed as they alighted from the carriage. Carlotta waited for the footman accompanying them to carry the picnic hamper. Ducks called as they made their way to a grassy spot near the river.

"Look at the ducks!" Beatrix called out, waving her hand for her sisters to join her at the edge of the river. Carlotta noticed how they were very careful not to get their shoes muddy.

"Here, try this." Carlotta reached into the hamper and pulled out a biscuit. She broke off a piece and handed a portion to each girl. "Toss it in."

The girls obeyed then squealed with delight when the ducks splashed and quacked, trying to get the free food before their comrades did.

"They must not like each other," Bethanny teased. Her beautiful face lighting up in a smile.

Carlotta tilted her head slightly, studying the young lady. She was not much younger than herself. With soft chestnut hair and beautifully deep eyes, Bethanny would draw the attention of many suitors. But not just yet, and for that, Carlotta was thankful, as she imagined the duke should be also. The young woman needed time to mend, to find herself after the painful loss of her parents. Time would help her heal, and then she'd have the strength to take London by storm.

After their lunch, they wandered Pultney Bridge and the shops that lined it. Careful to avoid the particular shops that could potentially recognize her, Carlotta steered her charges to different venues.

On their way back to Greenford Waters, Berty fell asleep, her sweet body resting against Carlotta as she rested peacefully.

"Thank you," Bethanny said quietly, her eyes sliding over to her sister's sleeping form.

"For?" Carlotta whispered.

"For today. I—I've had a governess before, Miss Lottie. Believe me when I say that none of them ever treated me as you do. For that I'm thankful."

"Of course... I'm happy to. But I don't think I'm any different from another governess." Carlotta spoke humbly.

"Yes, yes you are," Bethanny whispered, looking to Beatrix.

"Miss Lottie, our other governesses taught us well, just as you do. It's more of the way you are when you are *not* teaching us," Beatrix explained.

"Oh? And how is that?"

"You treat us as family."

Chapter Seven

"Charles, are you ready yet? I do think you take longer to depart than a green debutante. If I hadn't been suspicious that you fancied this governess of yours, I'd be convinced now." Lady Southridge spoke dryly as she waited in the library and Charles gave his footmen final instructions.

"Just because you arrive early doesn't give you the right to cast judgment," he ground out.

All morning his nerves had been frayed, his mind overworked with the anticipation and anxiety of seeing Carlotta again. His lack in ability to control his emotions was testing his patience and the last thing the needed was the dry sarcasm of Lady Southridge.

"I'm not an advocate of drinking spirits before noon, but I do think that perhaps you should have a glass of brandy, your eyes look positively wild."

"If I need brandy it's because I'll be in a carriage for the next two days with you," Charles muttered, but nevertheless poured himself a glass of brandy. Sipping it, he felt its warming trail to his stomach profoundly comforting. Taking a deep breath, he closed his eyes and forced his mind to focus.

"See? I knew it would help."

"Remind me again why you are coming?" Charles asked as he turned to face Lady Southridge.

"I was invited."

"I don't remember that part of our conversation." Charles raised an eyebrow. "I rather thought you invited *me* to my own estate. But that can't be accurate," he replied wryly.

"I distinctly remember my presence being necessary." She sniffed delicately.

"Which is far different than an invitation."

"Do you want me to explain, again, why I want to spend time with your wards? Because I'm surely able to list the reasons both you and Graham should have married by now producing Lord knows how many heirs given both your reputations," she challenged.

"I do believe I hear Murray. He must be coming to tell us the carriage is ready." Charles cleared his throat, his cravat seeming oddly tight. Lady Southridge's threat had hit its mark. The last thing he wanted to do was find himself in the middle of one of her matchmaking schemes.

Hearing about his ability to procreate was quite low on the list as well. Especially when approaching the topic with one viewed as a parent figure. Scratch that. It was definitely at the top of the list of things he never wanted to discuss, ever, with Lady Southridge.

Ever, *ever*.

However, he wouldn't mind discussing the topic with Carlotta.

He swallowed as he ducked into the hall. Murray wasn't anywhere to be found, but he hadn't expected to see him. He'd only mentioned him in desperation to change the subject of conversation.

He only hoped Lady Southridge didn't bring up the topic once they were in the carriage. He'd have no escape but to fling himself from the moving carriage.

But if she began speaking about his ability to produce offspring, he would be sorely tempted.

Charles walked a few steps down the hall, his mind wandering. It would take them almost two days to get to Greenford Waters. It was one of his favorite estates and its large landholding was the reason he sent the girls to that location. He had spent most of his boyhood in that home, and it carried fond memories for him still. It had been too long since he'd returned and he found himself anticipating their departure even more.

Of course, that Carlotta was in residence was an added siren call that couldn't be denied. He'd have to watch himself, closely. Not only did he not want to repeat the same mistakes he made earlier, but he'd have a witness: Lady Southridge.

The woman had a memory like an elephant.

Good Lord, this was going to be a nightmare.

"Your grace? The carriage is ready." Murray approached him from behind, bowing slightly.

"Very well. Please attend Lady Southridge. I'll meet her at the carriage."

Murray nodded and left, his back straight and tall as he walked to the library to alert Lady Southridge.

Charles strode to the circular drive where the carriage waited, pulled by his prized Blood Bays. The horses waited patiently, shaking their heads and chewing the bit.

Once seated in the well-sprung carriage, he closed his eyes.

"You're not fooling me. I know you're not asleep already. You aren't *that* old." Lady Southridge commented as she settled on the plush bench.

"Not sleeping, praying."

"For?"

"Deliverance."

She snorted.

"I do believe that was a snort. How unladylike," Charles

commented, opening his eyes and regarding her.

"When one speaks something so absurd, sometimes the only polite thing to do *is* snort. Any words I would have said would have been far less lady like." She shot back, a grin teasing her lips.

"Very well."

She leaned forward, as if about to disclose a great secret. "And for the record. I've been praying for deliverance as well... God keeps telling me to wait. At this point, I'm sure I'll be near death. But I have hope for you still."

"My heart beats with joy at your faith in me."

"Someone has to hold on to hope for your blackened soul," she quipped.

"How far is it to Bath, again?" Charles sighed heavily, glancing heavenward.

"As if you don't have the miles counted already. Less than two days, darling. If I were you, I'd worry less about enjoying my pleasant company and more about important matters."

"Such as?" Charles felt his eyebrow raise, his tone dubious.

"Such as whom you shall marry this season." She beamed and leaned back, her eyes bright with hope.

Bloody blooming damning hell.

"Swearing in your mind is just as much of a sin as speaking it out loud Charles," Lady Southridge chided. "Besides, do you really think I'm going to let you and Graham get away with your bachelor status for much longer? Both of you have a responsibility to produce an heir. I've reminded you both often enough that there is not a possible way you've forgotten, so I must simply assume that you need help." She leaned back, her expression full of assurance and... pity.

When one thought of hell, certainly fire, brimstone, and torture sprang to mind. The torture was indeed correct, but Charles was sure that hell looked a lot like his carriage and the devil looked like Lady Southridge.

"Don't look at me like that. It's the only possible conclusion." She shrugged delicately.

"I fail to see your logic," Charles whispered hoarsely. He was still recovering from the idea that Lady Southridge thought he needed… *help. Good Lord.*

"Neither you nor Graham seem to have the slightest inclination—"

"Ah-ha! You said inclination! That implies that we are choosing to, rather than doing so out of necessity! You're logic is faulty."

"You know it's rude to interrupt. I'll pretend you did not. As I was saying…" She pierced him with a steely glare. "While no one in London with ears can argue that you've had your fair share of… experience with women—"

"How delicately put." Charles grinned.

"When one is dealing with the decidedly indelicate, there is no other way to do it," she replied. "Are you finished interrupting? While we have two days, I'm not fond of continuing one topic of conversation the entire length of the trip."

"Forgive me, continue." Charles gestured to her, holding out his hand and nodding.

"Thank you. Now, as I was saying, while you certainly don't lack in the experience department, you do lack in the longevity department."

"I can—"

"I don't want to know." She gave him withering glare.

Charles chuckled. He was about to say that he had never once been told he lacked in the longevity department. Not once.

"I'm speaking of the length of your liaisons. They are abysmally short and not with the type of women that someone of your status should consider as a wife." She nodded.

Charles felt the humor drain from him. He wondered

what she'd think of the idea of him falling for a governess. However, she seemed to suspect it. Again, he was confused.

Blasted bloody woman.

Maybe she was jesting... perhaps she thought he was not sincerely at risk at falling for her. And if she were to learn the truth...

First, she'd think he was joking. Then she'd stare at him as if he had lost his mind. Which, he would have to wonder himself. After she got past the shock, she'd enter into a lengthy lecture on why it was completely insupportable.

He took a deep breath. He couldn't win. He was not to consort with the type of ladies that were readily available, nor could he be tempted to marry the one woman who seemed to manage that impossibility.

Hell.

"Charles? I do say, you've gotten quiet. Don't hurt yourself with all that thinking," Lady Southridge mocked.

Charles pulled his attention back to her. There was a slight smile in her eyes that negated the sarcasm in her voice.

"And what, pray tell, are you planning to do about all of this?" Charles asked. Better to get her plotting out in the open.

"This season, I'll compile a list of suitable women. Now, before you object—"

Charles had just opened his mouth,

"I will be very selective. You won't have to worry about a silly chit that thinks batting her eyelashes will land her a duke. No offense."

"None taken."

"But I know of a few ladies who would be fantastic matches for someone of your status and who can carry on intelligent conversation."

"Miracles do happen." Charles sighed.

"Indeed," Lady Southridge commented wryly.

****

The carriage ride was miserable, everlasting and Charles had seriously considered throwing his person from comfortable coach just to make the torture end. However, once he considered that his torture might just be beginning, should he end his life —after all, hell wasn't known for its luxury and peace and that's surely where he'd find himself— he considered throwing Lady Southridge from the carriage. She was light enough, but with his luck, she wouldn't die. Nope. She'd live, her legs and arms might not work but her mind, voice certainly would, and that would be far worse than any eternal carriage ride with her.

Funny how a person could love someone, yet still wish she would disappear.

Greenford Waters began to come into view and Charles exhaled the largest sigh he'd ever heard, from himself or anyone else for that matter.

"I haven't been *that* bad." Lady Southridge sniffed.

"Of course not," Charles responded, feeling much more charitable since the end was in sight.

"Well, I might have meddled some…" She waved a gloved hand as if it were a trivial matter.

"Some?" Charles felt his eyes widen and his jaw drop. *Some* was a gross and pathetic understatement.

"Well, yes."

"I seemed to have missed when you went from *some* to obscenely meddling. Or maybe I fell asleep and imagined you listing every deb this coming season and all their attributes, family history and shortcomings. Bloody hell, I do believe that was my worst nightmare ever." Charles spoke with thick sarcasm.

"No need to be short with me, Charles. I gave you fair warning. You and Graham must find suitable wives. You're not taking the job seriously, so I am offering my assistance."

"I also missed the part where you offered rather than

sentenced me."

"Sarcasm doesn't become you, Charles."

"I rather thought it made me dashing and dangerous. You know, what drives all the debutantes wild with wanting to redeem me from my sinful and cynical ways."

"You've deluded yourself."

"Here I thought I was the paragon of wisdom."

She sighed heavily. "If I didn't feel such a responsibility to care for you and Graham—"

"I relieve you of all responsibility."

She narrowed her eyes. "As I was saying. If I didn't feel such a responsibility for you and Graham, I would leave you to your wicked and worthless ways, but I find I cannot. Not when I have the power to help."

"God help me."

"I'll take that as a prayer."

"You may count it as such. I don't think I've ever whispered more reverent words in all my days."

She raised an eyebrow and turned her attention to the window. Greenford Waters was a beautiful stone mansion that had been in his family since the Tudors. It was solid and firm, like his title. Or so his father use to say. Just seeing the circular drive and the forest beyond brought back a million memories of his boyhood, eliminating the tension in the air from Lady Southridge's meddling.

"I forgot how beautiful it was here. Why don't you visit more often?" Lady Southridge asked quietly, almost reverently.

"London has its charms as well," he replied, but nothing felt further from the truth as he stared at the stately building, its marble steps, and perfectly manicured boxwoods.

"I doubt that."

"You'd be correct. I honestly don't know why I haven't been back for a while. Of all my estates, it's my favorite."

"You did grow up here."

"True."

"So it feels like home."

"I suppose you're correct."

The carriage halted just as the large front door opened. The estate's aged butler, Tibbs, stepped out followed by a flurry of footmen. The carriage door was opened and Tibbs helped Lady Southridge alight from the coach, her skirts swishing as she carefully stepped out. Charles exited next, inhaling deeply the salty sweet air. As the various footmen began unloading their belongings, Charles wondered if Carlotta and the girls had noticed his arrival.

Last week he had sent a missive to the housekeeper and Tibbs alerting them of his arrival, but had given explicit instructions that the governess and wards were not to be notified of his plans to visit. At the time, it seemed the wise thing to do; now he wondered. Certainly if Miss Lottie knew he were coming, she'd take the girls out for the day, or at least that's what he had worried. Now he thought that perhaps, that wouldn't have been a bad idea. It would have given him a chance to prepare himself.

He felt stronger, more able to resist the charms of the beautiful governess, but he didn't necessarily trust himself. He's self-control had been quite lacking before. Of course, he reasoned, that she had caught him off guard, in perhaps, a moment of weakness. But no longer.

Or so he hoped.

He nodded to Tibbs, who bowed at his entrance, and then headed directly to his study. Once there he poured himself a fortifying glass of brandy — the fortification was both necessary from the carriage ride with Lady Southridge and the upcoming reunion with the wards and Miss Lottie!

He studied the room that held the most memories of his father. Rich mahogany woods boasted power and elegance as well as strength. Crimson cushions and sapphire colored tapestries gave the distinct impression of wealth and royalty.

His father had prided himself in his heritage, the thick blood of nobility that had flowed through his veins, which continued to flow through Charles.

His father was like most dukes, he assumed. Present yet still absent. His childhood memories included his nannies, tutors and various kind servants, but few memories harbored images of his parents. Yet, he knew that if he had a strong need for them, they would have been there. Sadly, or maybe mercifully, he never had such an occurrence in his childhood that required such a response from them. But one thing he did remember about his father was his strength. That was why when he'd passed, over fifteen years ago, it had been quite shocking.

As a child, he never considered that his parents were mortal. That belief carried on into his young adulthood and somehow was still believed even as he passed his majority. A hunting accident. No glory, simply an accident stole the final heartbeats from his father's chest. His mother had been in London while his father hunted in Sussex that fateful day and upon hearing of her husband's demise, had taken it upon herself to alert their son.

Never had his mother appeared more fragile, less sure of herself. Always the perfect lady, she looked anything but when she arrived at Charles' London Town home.

Of course, a few months later he realized why she had appeared so weak. As he sat through her funeral service he wondered why he hadn't asked her about her health when he had the chance. But he was thinking of his father, of himself, not of her. And pneumonia claimed her with silent precision.

"Your grace?"

Charles startled slightly, glancing to his butler but not seeing him for a moment as his memories faded from the room and reality caught up with him once more.

"What is it, Tibbs?" he asked, his voice sounding overly weary to his own ears.

"You asked to be informed when the young wards and their governess arrived from their walk. They have just come in, your grace. And as you requested, they are not aware of your presence." Tibbs nodded obediently.

"Very good. See that I am the one to speak to them first, not, Lady Southridge."

"As you say, your grace." Tibbs bowed and turned to leave.

"Wait. On second thought, would you please bring Miss Lot—er, Carlotta to me, I wish to speak with her in private before the introductions begin.

Tibbs nodded then left.

Charles paced the study. A thousand thoughts filled his head, tempered by a few precious memories that set his blood to roaring. It was madness, to *feel* as he felt, after only such a short time. But it was there nonetheless. Perhaps it was just a passing fancy, he justified. There really was no reason for him to form such a strong attachment to the young governess in such short order. Perhaps all his emotional turmoil was for not. Could it be that in the amount of time passed, his attraction had cooled and he'd now not be as affected? He could only hope.

The sound of light footsteps reached his ears a moment before a knock came at the door.

"Come," Charles called, his eyes already searching for her face.

Tibbs entered followed by the source of Charles' sleepless nights; *Carlotta,* siren from his waking dreams.

It was too much to ask to be unaffected. It was too much to ask to even be *as* affected by her beauty as he was in the past.

No. All it took was one glance, one sweeping gaze from the soft golden curls on the top of her head to the slight peek of her slipped foot from her frock for him to lose all train of thought.

He hadn't even made eye contact yet.

Damn.

No, for everything he had hoped that time would dull the attraction, he had been deathly wrong.

For if anything, it had increased tenfold and as her clear green eyes searched his, it was all Charles could do to simply keep the fire ignited within him at bay.

Chapter Eight

"Your grace?" Carlotta asked, not quite believing her eyes. When Tibbs had requested her, he hadn't mentioned that the duke was in residence.

Come to think of it, he hadn't mentioned that the duke was coming to Greenford Waters at all.

Damn.

She felt her eyes widen as her cheeks blushed vermillion at her shock over her own thoughts. As if she spoke them out loud, she wished to cover her mouth and retreat, humiliated. Never before had she sworn, yet the duke seemed to provoke uncharacteristic reactions from her.

She should not be so surprised since he was the cause for various other reactions she hadn't previously experienced.

Staring at the deep furrow in his brow, she wondered if maybe she *had* spoken the curse aloud.

"Miss Carlotta." He nodded seriously, his expression shuttered and cool. As if a gaze could change the very temperature, she stifled a shiver. Already her heart was hammering in her chest, her lips tingling with the reminder that once, not so long ago, his had caressed them. Forcing her thoughts into submission, she took a step forward and curtseyed.

"That will be all Tibbs." The dear butler nodded but cast a wary glance to her as he retreated, leaving the door still open enough for propriety's sake.

"How are you and my wards adjusting to the country?" his grace asked with all the emotional attachment of a man inquiring about the weather.

"The adjustment has been minimal, your grace," Carlotta answered, the fact that he had simply called the girls his 'wards' chaffing against her. They deserved more than that. They did have names after all. But she supposed that was the way of it in his social circles. He was their benefactor, their protector so to say; emotional attachment wasn't a requirement.

"And you? How are you adjusting?" he asked. For but a moment his expression slipped to give her an insight into the simmering beneath the cool waters of his gaze, but just as quickly as it appeared, it was closed off.

"Well, your grace, Bath is quite close to where I was raised, so I find myself very much at ease here."

"I was not aware that you were from Bath." He seemed shocked that he hadn't been aware of that fact.

"Not Bath exactly, I was raise a few miles north, closer to the sea."

"Ah, do you have family? I could arrange for you—" He stopped his offer mid-sentence as she shook her head. "I see. My apologies if I have mentioned something to risk offending you." He bowed his head tenderly, completely confusing her from his earlier detached demeanor.

The man had more mood shifts than a play had scenes!

"It is of no consequence, your grace," Carlotta said, hoping to put the subject to rest. The last thing she wanted to do was discuss her history.

He nodded and then took a few steps about the room.

The silence was thick and heavy in the air, and Carlotta wanted to break it, but didn't know exactly how to go about doing just that. She had just opened her mouth to speak when the duke seemed to remember he had company.

"I have a guest here, a woman who accompanied me," he began.

Carlotta felt the blood drain from her face yet at the same time, she was thankful to have a reason to convince herself that their prior... interludes... were of not consequence. At least to him. This new knowledge would serve to remind her at night when she saw his alluring gaze in her dreams.

"I see. I'll be sure to tell the girls that you are not to be disturb—"

"Actually, I'm quite sure Lady Southridge will be more than happy to be 'disturbed' as you put it. I feel it necessary to explain that she feels a certain..." He paused as if thinking of the correct word. "...obligation to my wards."

"I shall do my best to make her feel welcome, then." Carlotta spoke bravely, all the while her mind spun in a million different directions. Had he brought this woman as a potential bride and she was already staking a claim on his wards? Was she mercenary in her intentions, sizing up the girls for their worth upon their majority? Maybe she was trying to get into his heart by showing compassion on those less fortunate. Either way the picture painted in her mind was one of shallow intentions and came from a jealous heart. Her own jealous heart.

"I have no doubts that you will do just that, Miss Carlotta." He nodded then resumed his infernal pacing.

And he was calling her Miss Carlotta, rather than Miss Lottie. It had not escaped her notice. She told her traitorous heart that it was another confirmation that he was simply telling her that whatever they had shared earlier was now in the past, over and finished. He no longer felt any attachment. Her heart pinched at the realization that she was so easily discarded, and disregarded. For her, kisses were so much more than frivolous tokens. To know they meant to little to him was stinging and hurtful.

Though these emotions all played havoc on her heart, she took great efforts to school her expression into one of polite disinterest. The same one she'd use when forced to be around whatever woman he brought to meet the girls.

"I don't think I've ever encountered you this quiet, Miss Carlotta."

She glanced up to find him watching her intently. The coolness of his gaze had warmed, like a loch heated by the summer sun, still chilly but refreshing and Carlotta felt herself losing ground.

"I, perhaps, do not have much to say, your grace," she replied.

"I, perhaps, find that hard to believe." He tilted his head in challenge.

"You are quite sure to believe what you wish, your grace," she replied, raising her eyebrow and issuing a challenge of her own.

He narrowed his eyes and watched her, the moments ticked by but she remained unmoved, unwilling to give away the secrets of her heart. Not to him.

Never to him.

At least never to him again.

"Damn it, Carlotta why don't you just say whatever is written all over your face? I cannot read your mind it is quite killing me right now."

"Why are you here?" she asked before she could sensor her words.

"It's my estate," he answered back.

"I'm pleased to add that to my growing information about you, your grace," she replied with a tart clip in her voice. Her self-control was slipping in light of his likewise lack of emotional control and she began to resort to her wit in order to keep to safer subject matter.

"Did I just mention that you were quiet? I take back my erroneous statement," he said dryly.

At this, Carlotta couldn't help the small smile that teased her lips.

"And quit that insufferable smirking," he groused. " If you must know, I'm here because I was forced to make an appearance."

"I find that hard to believe, your grace." Carlotta felt her eyebrows shoot up at his declaration. Just who was this woman who had accompanied him? What hold did she have on his heart for him to jump at her whim?

"There are forces of nature you have never encountered," he replied dryly. "Lady Southridge is one of those forces of nature, Miss Lottie, and I don't pity you that you'll be quite in the middle of her raptures."

"I'm afraid I don't understand." Carlotta paused, even as her heart rejoiced that he slipped into calling her 'Miss Lottie.'

" Lady Southridge is my good friend's sister and, much to my dismay, has determined that same office over myself. And, through some means I am still not aware, she learned that I had inherited three wards and I had no choice but to accompany her here to provide introductions. I had no free will in the matter."

"Oh, then we shall do our best to meet whatever requirements she has for the girls so that you may be free to leave," Carlotta replied carefully.

"I have no qualms about staying here, Miss Carlotta, but I do have qualms about her staying her for an indefinite duration, which I'm sure she's planning at this very moment."

Not knowing how to respond, Carlotta simply nodded.

"And I wanted to speak with you before she pounced, so you would be aware of the situation and encourage the wards to be kind."

"I assure you the *girls* will be all that is goodness and

light, your grace." Carlotta replied in a clipped tone.

"I—"

"And they are girls, not simply wards." Carlotta finally spoke the words she had wanted to shout from the first moment he had reduced them to simply an obligation rather than the delight that they were. Her tone was soft but steely, and she prayed she hadn't offended him... too much.

He stared at her, as if weighing his next words. Anger had flushed his face yet his eyes were calculating as if his mind were trying to convince his emotions to back down.

So she waited, her hands clasped in front of her and her posture prim and straight.

"Be that as it may..." he began, then paused, working his jaw and narrowing his eye slightly, "I still *require* you to indulge Lady Southridge's whims.

"Of course, your grace. Is there anything else?" Carlotta asked as she kept her posture stiff.

"Yes. So please, make yourself comfortable. I'm nowhere finished with you yet." He gestured to the settee, a rebellious smile tilting his lips and making him appear the rake his reputation had deemed.

Carlotta bit the inside of her lip, then walked to the settee and sat, a sigh escaping her lips.

"Tsk, tsk, Miss Lottie. We cannot have you give a bad example to the *girls*. You shouldn't sigh so." He shook his head.

"Forgive my sigh, your grace." She smiled, knowing she was playing a dangerous game to provoke him, yet she couldn't seem to restrain herself.

"All is forgiven. I had not known my presence was so exasperating," he commented as he dusted imaginary lint from his sapphire colored waistcoat.

"I value honestly over flattery, your grace."

"Touché, Miss Lottie. It seems you are in possession of a sharp wit this afternoon. I will simply have to hone my own in order to give you a worthy counterpart."

"There is no need—"

"Oh, indeed there is." His eyes took on a predatory gleam as he stepped forward slowly, deviously, and challengingly.

Carlotta watched his approach with growing suspicion. Whatever he was about was not good.

"Perhaps to conquer your wit, I'll simply have to silence it," he mused, his gaze roaming her features. Gone was the cool displeasure of earlier, replacing it was a warm and teasingly passionate expression that lit Carlotta's stomach to fluttering and her blood to pulsing furiously through her veins. His gaze moved from hers to settle upon her lips. Though the glance was quick, it changed the depth of his eyes from a summer lake's blue to the passionately tousled North Sea's hue in the midst of a storm. Hunger burned brightly, stealing all thought from Carlotta's captivated mind.

"Yes, I see that if I'm to conquer you at your own game, I must change the rules."

"I don't think—"

"Thinking would be a very bad idea right now," he whispered, holding his hand out as he paused before her.

Glancing to his hand, she paused, debating. She could feel his body heat and it called to her, beckoned her. The scent of cinnamon and cloves permeated the air, thickening it, weaving a spell around her till she felt her hand reach for his. Immediately his grip tightened and he pulled softly, and she stood. Though she only came up to his chin, it seemed the perfect height for his scent to hold her captive, for his eyes to penetrate her soul.

As if he knew she were about to try and break the spell that passion had woven so intricately around them, he silenced her unspoken efforts with his lips. Softly, his lips met hers, but with determined pressure, he left no question that this kiss was very, very intentional.

Though chaste by most standards, this kiss seemed to

place his claim on her soul. After the brief touch, he leaned back gazing into her eyes, eyes she realized, had never closed through the short duration of the kiss.

His gaze spoke the question clearly, though words were never used.

Again?

Carlotta felt herself nod ever so slightly, but it was all the confirmation the duke needed for his lips captured hers once more.

And this kiss was far from chaste.

His lips caressed hers with a persuasion she was unable to deny. She inhaled deeply, letting the moment flood her senses. His taste of peppermint combined with his masculine and heady scent of cinnamon was nearly her undoing. He teased her lips with his tongue, caressing them before biting gently and evoking the most astonishing pleasure she had ever encountered.

As if of their own accord, her arms found their way to embracing him, his solid shoulders were warm beneath her gloved hands and firm in their strength. His muscles were coiled, roped in a way that was completely primal and she wantonly desired to be able to feel him far more than her gloves and his jacket allowed.

His hands pressed into the small of her back, guiding her deeper into his embrace. Warm tingles of delight danced in her belly as his lips left hers and traveled across her jawline to her ear.

"You taste sweeter than I remember. How I utterly missed you," he whispered, causing Carlotta to gasp at the revelation.

He had missed her?

Well he *was* kissing her... so that signified.

But somehow hearing it from his lips, and then having those same lips *show* just how much his words were true.

It was delightful.

Splendid.

Utterly—

"Charles?" a woman's voice called, her footsteps becoming louder as she undoubtedly made her way down the hall.

Immediately breaking the kiss he cast a frightened glance to the open door then back to her. His eyes were still drunk with passion and slightly unfocused as if his mind were trying to pull itself from the blazing haze their kissing had created.

"Bloo—blasted woman. I should have tossed her from the carriage when I had the chance." The duke spoke in a frustrated whisper. He glanced to the door, then to her, then back to the door.

"Charles? I say, where could he have gone?"

"Hide."

"Excuse me?" Carlotta stammered, not quite believing her ears... or her eyes for that matter, for the duke was pulling her by the hand to hide behind a large tapestry.

"Hide! She can't see you. Not yet."

"You can't be serious!" Carlotta exclaimed as he all but shoved her behind the heavy curtain.

He covered her mouth with his hand, the warmth of his skin seeping through her lips and warming her core, causing a hum of desire to reawaken within her.

"You must be quiet. She'll hear you and... I'm not prepared to deal with this just yet."

She was confused, but with his warm hand covering her mouth, she couldn't really question his strange statement.

"Do not move." His gaze was firm, decided and Carlotta felt herself nod in agreement though she had no idea why.

"Very good." With quick spin on his heel, he covered her within the confines of the tapestry. A swirl of dust motes danced in the air in his wake. She sent up a quick prayer she'd not sneeze.

Chapter Nine

"Charles! There you are!" Lady Southridge breezed into his study uninvited. Though he wasn't surprised. He exhaled sigh of relief that Carlotta was safely hidden away, and close. Though he began to question the wisdom in hiding her within listening distance of Lady Southridge. This could be bad.

Very bad.

But of course that hadn't crossed his mind three minutes ago.

No, that would have been to bloody convenient.

"Charles, I say, where is that governess of yours?"

"Lady Southridge, might I suggest that you take a moment of respite in your rooms from our long journey?" He appealed sweetly.

"What are you about Charles?" She speared him with a gaze that was penetrating to his very bones. Like a young boy caught with his hand in the plum pudding, he felt caught in his own trap. But there was no way to go but through it.

"Why, Lady Southridge, I thought you'd be impressed with my consideration of your delicate sensibilities." He bowed with a flourish, mostly to hide the smile from Lady

Southridge's view. *Delicate sensibilities, Ha!*

"Are you feeling quite well, Charles? You looked... flushed."

"Quite well, my lady." Charles cleared his throat.

"I see... about this governess. I have not seen her and your servants are quite unhelpful I must say. I wish to speak with her. How am I to determine character—"

"Lady Southridge, I'm sure that she is occupied at the present. She does have three wards to care for."

"Speaking of which, I did get to meet your wards." Lady Southridge's face transformed. Her earlier pinched expression lit up, causing her face to break into a rapturous smile. "Lovely young ladies, Charles. I cannot believe you were able to separate yourself from them for so long. Their manners are impeccable and all three of them will set Town on fire upon their come-out. I cannot wait." She sighed in delight.

"I—"

"Don't even think of denying me this privilege, Charles. I'll not have it." She shrugged a shoulder delicately, but her gaze was ironclad, making her will quite clear.

Charles sighed. He'd deal with this later. What he needed to do was get rid of Lady Southridge from his study so that Carlotta could come out of hiding.

He paused, determining his plan. "Why don't you spend some more time with the wards then, Lady Southridge. I'm sure you have much that you'd be able to teach them." Charles was proud of his bait; surely she'd take it and leave.

"Perhaps you're right... but I wonder, where is their governess? It seems she was summoned by your butler... Charles." She narrowed her eyes and took a determined step forward.

"Yes?" Charles resisted the urge to back up, or loosen his cravat, really anything to take her gaze from inspecting his own.

"What did you do with her?" Lady Southridge asked

with an all too deceptive calm. Her gaze then left his and began to study the room.

"I have done anything." *That I'd dare tell you.* He added silently, thus making his lie more of a truth At least that's what he told himself.

Her eyes widened and Charles panicked.

"What a lovely view! I had all but forgotten that your grounds are so high. I can see part of Bath from here." She stepped towards the window, her eyes focused on the view outside.

Charles' heart hammered, he forgot to breathe. Of course, Lady Southridge would approach the window right next to Carlotta.

Fate really should be so cruel.

Or maybe he should have not hidden her at all.

But the real question was, did Lady Southridge *know* Carlotta was hiding and was simply was toying with him, or was she truly oblivious? Charles scanned the tapestries, there was no bulge, and since the cloth touched the floor, no dainty slipped foot could be seen peeking out.

The stress was killing him.

As if to confirm his anxious state, a drop of perspiration trickled down his temple.

And it wasn't even warm in the room.

"Has your governess taken the girls to Bath? I would love to accompany them... perhaps tomorrow. That is, if we can find her. I do say Charles, for one so smitten, you really are quite unaware of her person," she chided.

Charles closed his eyes, praying that perhaps Carlotta would have missed that very loud statement of Lady Southridge's. He felt his face color, his humiliation compounded by her next statement. " I say, for her to have you in such a lather, I'd of thought you'd seek her out immediately, yet here I find you... alone... you *are* alone... aren't you Charles?" she asked, her gaze piercing him as if she could lift the answer from his mind.

"Actually... I am *not* alone. You are in my company, Lady Southridge... It would be quite neglectful of me to not acknowledge your presence," he responded with his usual wit, but his voice sounded strange, strained.

As if smelling his deception, she sniffed then narrowed her eyes.

"That goes without saying, Charles. I'm quite aware of my own person. I'm not senile... yet," she added with a slight smile.

She turned to the window once more, her slight smile growing.

It was the cat and mouse game. One Charles had enjoyed playing more than once before... but he was always the cat. Never the mouse.

However, right now he was the mouse.

And Lady Southridge was a very large cat. Who looked very much like she had just eaten the canary.

Clearing his throat, Charles reached up to loosen his cravat. *Blast it all it was sweltering in that room!*

"If you are so set on finding Miss Lottie then I'll call Tibbs, surely he will help you locate her."

Lady Southridge sighed. "That will not be necessary." She eyed him meaningfully.

Charles swallowed hard. Holding his breath, he waited.

"I'll simply retire for a few moments and then I'm sure I'll find her quite easily. She must have simply stepped out. Even governesses need fresh air." She spoke graciously all while eyeing him meaningfully.

If he could only figure out what her *meaningful* glance meant.

"Very well, I'll not detain you."

She left quietly, her skirts swishing as she departed. Charles exhaled the breath he had held until she was out of sight, then he leaned against his desk, his heart sill pounding.

Turning he strode to the window.

"Charles?" Lady Southridge's voice startled him, causing him to jump and turn, his eyes large and his pride quite wounded at such a response.

"I do say... are you quite well? You're quite agitated. Perhaps I shouldn't leave," she mused.

"I'm well, quite well. What is it you needed?" he asked, forcing his demeanor to its usual poise.

"I was simply going to ask at what time we dine? Country hours are usually different than that of Town, you know."

"Six thirty," he responded curtly, annoyed that her further intrusion was for such a trivial matter.

"Very fashionable, Charles." She nodded then left, but not before she cast a curious glance to the window as if something she saw there was not quite right... but she was unable to determine just what.

"I'll see you at dinner. It will be quite informal as I'm assuming you'll wish the girls to dine with us," Charles offered, trying to steal her attention away from the window.

Desperation was nipping at his heels.

"Delightful. I shall look forward to it. And you're sure your well?" Her gaze swept over him with concern.

"Perfectly splendid."

"Very well." She gave him once last glance that spoke of her lack of convincing, but she departed nonetheless.

Miracles do happen.

However, just to be safe, he waited till he heard her footsteps fade from the hall.

Then he went and shut the door.

Then locked it for good measure.

Then just to be sure, he put the key in his pocket and waited one minute more.

"I *believe* it's safe now, Miss Lottie," he called out; his nerves were shot.

Carlotta threw the tapestry away from her person and stormed out of hiding, her face flushed and her hair askew from the rubbing of the rough cloth against it.

"Hide? You have me *hide?*" she asked, her color bright and her eyes sparking with defiance and indignant anger.

Charles had never seen her more beautiful.

Really, he should have stayed in London.

"I wasn't thinking rationally, I must admit." He rubbed the back of his neck.

"Surprising."

"Sarcasm with a smile. I must add that talent to your growing list of attributes," he retorted, but his face broke into a grin.

It wasn't that funny. But the tension from the previous situation was draining from him leaving him slightly unhinged.

Or maybe it was just her.

"Never in all my life have I been asked to *hide* from someone! If I cause you that much humiliation that you cannot even have me in the same room—"

"Hush now, little kitten. Retract those claws and cease your hissing." Charles chuckled even as he noted her cheeks filled with a deepening reddish hue as he did so. "I'm not ashamed of you... however since our... conversation was more intimate than I was comfortable with in allowing for introductions, I admit my sense left me and I resorted to juvenile behavior." He took a step towards her, unable to resist the furious flush of her countenance.

Carlotta sniffed indignantly, crossing her arms and then uncrossing them so she could tuck the stray strands of hair released from her proper style behind her dainty ears.

Her color faded into more of her natural rosy elegance and Charles relaxed, risking another step forward.

"I must ask you to stop, your grace." She spoke softly, her eyes limpid pools of untapped passion that Charles very greedily wanted to explore.

But he obeyed and held his position.

"You... I'm not..." she began then hesitated, tucking more free strands of hair behind her ears. The gesture made her appear vulnerable and Charles felt a strange yet overwhelming desire to protect her from whatever caused her wariness.

Even if it meant protecting her from himself.

Strange irony, that.

"Yes?" he prodded, his voice gentle in comparison to the war waging within him. All he wanted to do was devour her, taste her addicting flavor once more... yet he would not. As much as he wanted, no, burned for her, he'd rather feel the flames lick his feet than cause her distress.

Lord knows he'd already caused enough.

And the day wasn't even over yet.

Bloody Hell

But it was more than that. He was thinking about her, concerned for her, putting aside himself and his own desires... for her. The idea stopped him short. Truly, he couldn't remember ever feeling this way before.

Which wasn't exactly complimentary.

But he disregarded that epiphany, reverting back to the first truth. For the first time Charles felt that he might actually, truly be falling in love.

Real love.

The kind where he would actually look *forward* to waking up beside that person for the rest of his life, rather than wanting to leave immediately after his lust was sated.

The kind where he would find the other person more attractive with silvery hair, and fine lines around her eyes from smiling too many times in his presence.

The kind that required a ring. Not simply a bed.

"Your grace?" Carlotta's hand on his arm jolted him from his thoughts.

"Forgive me," he whispered, his voice soft as he was still considering all he just uncovered within his own heart.

"There's nothing to forgive..." She arched an eyebrow. "At least in the past few minutes."

"I cannot think of anything today I'd ask forgiveness for," he challenged back.

Her cheeks bloomed with rosy color. "Including when you asked me to hide?" She tilted her head slightly, her eyes dancing with the knowledge that she had bested him.

"Perhaps that... but *only* that." He gave her his best smoldering gaze.

But her eyes didn't dance with invitation as he had hoped. Rather they grew wary once more and she backed away, her arms crossing once again as if trying to give herself security.

Charles swallowed his impulse to kiss the worry from her expression; rather he relaxed on his back leg and waited.

"You cannot keep insisting on kissing me, your grace. There will be talk, there will be consequences and I will come out with the unfavorable end, to be sure."

"Carlotta—" he began but hesitated as she lifted her gloved hand for him to wait.

"Your grace. We have already established that this—" She gestured between the two of them. "—is not wise. For pity's sake, you're a *duke*. I might simply be a governess but I'm not unaware of how your social circles work. While I'm assured that you are most certainly aware of how incompatible any type of relationship beyond employer and employee would be, I feel compelled to add..." She paused with a soft sigh, her eyes closing as if humbled beyond what she could bear. "...I'm not one to consider *carte-blanche*."

Her eyes were still closed.

Charles heart sank lower than hell itself.

Was that what she thought?

Granted his reputation didn't add any shine to his

character, but he had hoped she saw beyond... but apparently, he was incorrect.

"I do not remember asking you to be my mistress," Charles said, keeping his voice deceptively calm.

"I didn't wish to give you the opportunity. Such a... humiliation I could not bear, not at your hand," she whispered, her eyes opening and her expression lacerating through his heart like a jagged and rusty knife.

"The wards will be searching for you, Miss Carlotta. You best seek them out," his tone was cold, cruel to his own ears. He resented himself the moment he spoke but it was done.

It was done.

Silently he opened the door, steeping back for her to take her leave. He willed his expression to remain neutral, fighting the deep emotion suffocating him, emotion he couldn't name nor did he want to explore.

At least not at the moment.

"Very well." She curtseyed and quit the room but not before he saw the sheen of tears well within her eyes.

Charles waited till her footsteps vanished from hearing and then he closed his study door. He leaned against it, banging his head on the hard wood, praying for a punishment worse than the simple headache he'd have later.

Why did he send her off like that? All he had done was affirm that her opinion of him was correct. Hell, if he were a spectator in the tragedy that was now his life, he would have wanted to pummel himself. But no, his wicked blasted pride got in the way the moment she spoke of mistresses.

Little did she know that he hadn't had one in quite a while. Not since her. And even the *thought* of her as a mistress... it caused his blood to race yet spike with a dangerous pitch. It raced for the knowledge what would take place if she *were* his mistress, and it spiked in thinking that she'd be nothing more.

Mistresses were ignored when their... *service* wasn't

necessary.

Mistresses were paid company.

Mistresses were never married. Ever.

And Charles would fight the devil himself if another gentleman ever thought of bringing her under his *protection*. Which inevitably happened with mistresses. A man grew bored with one, so he traded in for another, leaving the previous mistress to find a new protector.

To think of Carlotta in such a state, it made his blood run cold. And his fists ached to beat someone.

Too bad right now the only person to blame was himself. He couldn't rightly call *himself* out.

What a bloody mess.

"Charles?" Lady Southridge's voice called to him.

Just for good measure, he thumped his head a few more times against the door. If he passed out then he wouldn't have to speak with her... he could claim temporary memory loss and forget that the disaster that just happened with Carlotta didn't even happen. Better yet, he could hit his head hard enough to actually cause memory loss and he'd be ignorant.

But alas, fate was never kind... at least to him.

"Charles?"

"Here. In hell. Come join me," he responded as he backed away and pulled open his study door.

"What on earth are you doing? And what is that odd thumping noise?" Lady Southridge asked as she regarded him with some alarm.

"Me beating myself. Come, I'm feeling especially charitable and I'll give you a stick so that you might join in the fun," he muttered.

"What did you do now?" Lady Southridge shook her head and made herself comfortable on the settee.

The same settee where Carlotta sat.

"Charles... are you particularly fond of this piece of furniture? If it upsets you so, I will not..."

"No, no. Please sit." He shook his head and trudged over to the chair near the fire.

"I met your Miss Carlotta." Lady Southridge leaned forward, her eyes bright and... knowing.

"Delightful." Charles tried to muster a proper response but he couldn't find the strength.

"I must say, I expected more of a response. I'll have to try harder. Perhaps you can help me. You see... I caught up with her as she was leaving this very hallway, her eyes suspiciously red rimmed."

"You don't say," Charles replied dryly.

"Indeed. In fact..."

Charles stared into the fire, waiting for her to begin her inquisition.

"I do believe she was foxed!" Lady Southridge's eyes were wide with conviction.

"Foxed?" Charles swung around to face her, his jaw dropping in shock. "Foxed you say?" he repeated again.

Such an outrageous thought needed repeating.

Rather, it probably *shouldn't* have been repeated. Or stated in the first place.

"Foxed," she said again, her head nodding in affirmation.

"She was not foxed." Charles felt compelled to defend.

"How can you be sure? Why, you'd be shocked at how many servants—"

"I'm quite aware of what servants do when they feel no one is watching... my own valet has sampled my French brandy a time or two... but Car—Miss Carlotta wouldn't. I'm sure of it."

"But how can you be so sure?" Lady Southridge asked, her arms folded.

"Because... she just wouldn't." Charles huffed indignantly.

"And that is all the credibility you can give to the subject?" she asked.

"No. But that's all I'm willing to share on the subject." Charles stood and paced in front of the fire.

"I shall investigate myself." Lady Southridge shrugged and stood as if to leave.

"You will do no such thing. You will not even *mention* that you thought so ill of her, let alone investigate her. You will leave her alone. Am I understood?" He spoke with a steel edge to his voice, one he couldn't ever remember using on Lady Southridge.

"My, you are in knots over this girl... I had expected it of course but... hmm." She paused and regarded him. "The only other explanation I can think of for her countenance was tears. But of course... you'd never make her cry... would you, Charles?" Lady Southridge didn't move and her expression remained unaltered.

But Charles smelled the blood in the water.

His own blood.

And she was a circling shark that had just trapped its prey.

Pity the prey was him.

"I—"

"Because if a gentleman cares for a lady... regardless of her station... she should never have cause for tears." Lady Southridge began to circle about the room. Walking to the same window, she lightly touched the tapestry where Carlotta had hidden only minutes ago.

Apparently, she wasn't joking about her suspicion of his affection for Carlotta. He was taken off balance by the full realization that Lady Southridge was championing her, siding with her.

Against him.

If Lady Southridge approved...

"I'm not quite as ignorant as you might imagine Charles," she commented lightly.

Charles closed his eyes in both humiliation and prayer.

His reverent yet soundless whispers to the Almighty begged for the ground to swallow him.

Better yet, swallow Lady Southridge.

He opened one eye just in case, but nothing.

Damn.

Lady Southridge continued to watch him, studying him with far more awareness and likely accuracy than he appreciated. But there was nothing to do but wait it out.

"So tell me, what are your reservations?" Lady Southridge spoke curiously.

"Reservations?"

"I've not been living on a rock, Charles. While your conquests of late," she said, eying him meaningfully, "are of the more notorious variety. You've never been one to hide your nature... or your actions. At least from anyone who would have the courage to ask."

"What are you getting at?" Charles snapped, losing his patience.

"That there must be something about this governess that you find so necessary to keep secret that you resort to hiding her behind curtains to keep her from view. And in all my time in knowing you... which has been a very long time indeed, I have never known you to hide anything... even that which is shameful and you rather *should* hide." Her eyes widened as she spoke the last phrase, her tone wry and reproachful.

"You think I'm ashamed of her?" Charles asked dubiously.

"I'm quite certain of it... and if my instincts are correct, I imagine she feels somewhat similar." She raised an eyebrow.

"Of all the..." Charles ran his fingers through his dark hair, resisting the urge to pull it out.

Women.

"I was trying to *protect* her! Not just hide her for my own... I don't even want to speculate what answer you could come up with." He blew out a frustrated breath.

"Protect her? From whom?" Lady Southridge asked, disbelief in her tone.

"You."

"Pardon?" she asked, her eye narrowing.

And this is why I hid her...

"Restraint is not in your repertoire, Lady Southridge. You would have seen her and pounced."

"I'm not a house cat, Charles," she replied bitterly, and with an ungracious acknowledging shake of her head.

"I'd compare you more to a lioness myself," he teased.

"So *I'm* to blame? I find this a little farfetched." She sniffed indignantly.

"For the hiding... yes." Charles nodded then turned to face the fire, hoping his answer would eliminate her further questions.

He really should have known better.

"Then why, pray tell, did the poor creature dissolve into tears once I left? I said nothing." She paused as if remembering her words. "Very well, I might have not been the soul of discretion but I didn't say anything that would cause tears. Of that I'm sure."

He remained silent.

"Charles," Lady Southridge warned.

"You haven't even met her, why are you on her side?"

"I'm not about *sides* I'm about finding you a suitable wife!"

"I don't need your help!"

"Yes you do! She ran from the room crying!"

"I don't *want* your help!"

"You don't get a choice."

"And this is why I hid her from you!"

"Because you don't want me to ruin your chances?"

"No I just—"

"You what, Charles," Lady Southridge snapped back.

"I didn't want her to face your disapproval." There, he

said it. And already he felt miserable.

"Disapproval?" Lady Southridge repeat, her tone shocked and hurt.

"Must I repeat myself?" he answered tiredly.

"No. I believe you were perfectly clear. Upon my word, Charles. Is this how you treat her?"

"No, I treat her much worse, apparently. After all, I did dissolve her to tears only a moment before you arrived. And here *you* stand, completely tearless... I must try harder," he replied sarcastically, with venom.

"Anger will get you nowhere, Charles. The truth however, might have some promise."

"I told you the truth."

"No, you told me a portion. The real question is... *why* would I not approve?" she asked, her head tilted thoughtfully.

"Must you truly ask that?"

"Apparently."

Charles felt his shoulders sag; his body weary from traveling now seemed almost as if it were full of lead rather than blood. And lucky him, this was the day that would last for eternity.

"Because... she's a bloody governess! Do you want the truth? I'm miserably wretched for her because I *know* I'm not good enough for her. My title, my money, my connections. Nothing of it is worth a farthing because it matters not in the truest of things. She is far better than I, yet I cannot pursue her because a match between us is insupportable because I'm a duke... and far poorer in character than she deserves." Charles walked numbly to the chair closest to the fire and sank into it, sagging his head to be cradled in his hands.

"Oh." Lady Southridge's voice grated on his last fraying nerve.

He had just bared his bloody wretched and blasted —and any other apprehensible adjectives relevant— soul to the miserable woman and all she could say was *"oh"*?

All he wanted was a never-ending decanter of brandy and to forget today existed.

Ever.

Ever. Ever.

Expect for that kiss.

That he wished to remember... simply nothing else of the mess that followed.

"Charles?" Lady Southridge's voice pulled him from the pool of self-pity in which he was currently swimming.

"Yes?" he asked, his voice muffled by his hands as they still held his head.

"You are an idiot."

"Your support is overwhelming. As each moment passes I'm increasingly thankful I brought you along," he replied toneless.

"You should be thankful I'm here to fix the miserable mess you call your life. To think, you, a rake. Ha! I laugh at such outrageous claims. You, sir, have no clue about women or love or anything beyond what takes place between the sheets." She *tsked* her tongue.

"I do believe your language was not becoming of a lady," he said dryly.

"I do believe that your behavior is abhorrent. However, there is hope for you still."

"I'm glad someone is of that conviction. I, myself, am contemplating other options."

"Never can expect brilliance from a duke."

"I have no response to that statement in my current state, but I *will* think of an excellent reply which I will unleash and fillet you with later." Charles glanced up at her, a scowl firmly in place.

"My heart quivers." She put her hand up to her forehead, mockingly. "So... the almighty Duke of Clairmont has fallen. I do believe it is a time for miracles to abound. And before you make any more snide comments—" She held up a hand as he made to open his mouth. "—while she is a governess... I have reason to believe that she is not *just* a governess. I made a few inquiries while we were in London. What I can't believe is that you did so little research into her background."

"She came to us on excellent recommendation," Charles defended.

"Yes, from her solicitor, Mr. Burrows."

"No, my solicitor."

"Hers as well. How do you think she knew of the opening so quickly?"

Actually, he had never thought that deeply about the subject.

"Why in the world would Carlotta have a solicitor?"

"Why indeed?" Lady Southridge raised an eyebrow.

"You obviously have some knowledge of which I'm not aware of... yet. Are you inclined so share or must I be left in suspense?"

"I'm considering suspense, but I'm going to take pity on you."

"I do appreciate being pitied."

She gave him a withering glare.

"I have a question that is a prerequisite for my discloser of information."

"Delightful."

"I want to meet her first."

"That's not a question. Regardless, the answer is no."

"Then I'll keep my information."

"Damn it."

"Such language!"

"We both know you are not shocked. Don't pretend that I offended your delicate sensibilities. We both know those do not exist either."

"You are in fine form," she remarked none too gently.

"You have provoked me to that place, Madam,"

"Please. I wish to meet her." Her tone was quiet,

pleading.

And completely out of character.

"Why?"

"Because I want to."

"In the light of such persuasive argument, I must reconsider," he replied dryly.

"Charles, you cannot imagine how long I have waited and hoped against all odds that you might be capable of love."

"Your faith in me is humbling."

"If you had seen your life from my perspective, I don't think you'd come to any different of a conclusion. But now I find myself realizing that hope, that there truly is a woman able to ensnare your attention to the point of idiotic behavior that is vastly unlike you under normal circumstances. Based on what I know of her, she is unlikely to be a fortune hunter. If she is a governess, she'd be well aware that her chances of attracting the matrimonial attitude of a man of quality are slim. Especially that of a duke. And *if she were trying to* trap you, I'm quite sure you'd smell that plan a mile away. After all, you have been fighting off those type of women since the cradle."

"Carlotta is *not* a fortune hunter. She doesn't..." He trailed off, not sure if he wanted to disclose his intimate knowledge with Lady Southridge.

"She doesn't... what, Charles?" She waited patiently, her expression open but Charles knew the curiosity was likely eating her alive.

"It's of no import."

"I find that difficult to swallow. The truth, if you please." She held out her hand magnanimously.

"I swear, *this, this* emotional upheaval is why men pity others of our sex who have fallen in love. Never have I had so much need for brandy in all my life." He shook his head and leaned back in his chair, closing his eyes as he rested his head against the back cushion.

"This sounds promising."

Charles didn't speak.

"I will continue to poke and prod the subject till you tell me, this is your fair warning."

"You are a miserable wretch."

"I'm still waiting."

"She doesn't even want me. *That*, is how I know she isn't a fortune hunter. And she's not playing coy either. I could easily see through that masquerade. But no, the woman I finally think could reform my wicked ways wants nothing to do with them. Though if I were in her position, I'd likely make the same choice. It's far wiser. I have nothing save a title and money to offer her. While that would be far more than what most women would desire in a husband, that and, if I say so myself, I'm quite dashing and handsome..." He grinned wryly, though his heart ached. His attempt at humor fell flat to his own ears.

"So, let me see if I have grasped the situation correctly."

"Yes, please summarize my pathetic existence. I'd love to hear it from your gracious perspective. And I thought the day couldn't get worse," he mumbled.

"Life is what you make of it. You, of all people, have no excuse. You've been given everything. Don't be so pathetic to find something, *someone* that requires far more effort on your part and only roll over and quit. *You* are better than that, Charles."

"Is that what you think I'm doing? Giving up? I'm here aren't I? Believe me, I was trying, *trying* to do the noble thing and keep myself away! Then you had to barge into my life, inject yourself into the middle of my dilemma and now here I stand, completely at odds with all that I thought I was doing that was correct and I find I was wrong? I can't pursue her! I can't offer for her, and I'll not degrade her with offering less. Nor will I tolerate you inspecting her like a brood mare. I don't even feel as though I make sense any longer." He stood up abruptly and paced about the room.

"Sit, Charles."

"I'm not your pet."

"No, you're like my son, and while you are doubting my intentions, I promise you that there is a solution and one that will find you quite happily able to pursue your governess. Now, will you please sit and cease your infernal pacing?"

Charles glared, but sat.

"Now. Before you introduce me, I need you to understand something. While your title does put certain… obligations… on your future wife, those are not set in concrete. Your claim that you cannot pursue her based on her position is nothing short of being a coward. So that excuse is no longer valid. Next—"She paused, subjecting Charles to a very patient glare. "You must choose if you truly desire this woman. I can see, based on your testimony of her virtues, that she is no light skirt or one to dally with. You must choose your words and ways wisely. Under your employ, she will be put in a very difficult position should you choose to try and win her affections. Finally—"

"Will this ever end?" Charles lamented.

"Yes, now quiet yourself so I may finish. Finally, if what I learned is correct, your Miss Lottie is actually Carlotta Standhope whose father was a baron. Titled, but barely. The information I was able to accumulate on such short notice also spoke of a loss of income that precluded her seeking employment. Rumors had it that she was expecting to go to London for a season next year."

"A season? Carlotta planned a come out?"

"Yes."

Charles' imagination quickly spun into action as he dreamed of watching her enter from across the room. Her golden hair spun up and her pastel colored gown clinging to all her perfect curves. The sound of her bell-like laughter carrying across the room to his waiting ears. She'd glance over and meet his gaze…

"Charles? Now is not the time for your wild imagination."

"Excuse me?" He shook his head.

"What I'm trying to explain is that your chances at winning the affections of your governess, which I might add, I still have not had the pleasure of meeting, are quite good. This of course is on the assumption that you can woo her properly."

"I can woo."

"Yes, her earlier behavior was solid evidence."

"I—"

"You have no excuse. Now. Will you please introduce me to the woman who has succeeded in tying you in knots? It's been such a dream of mine. I find myself afraid she doesn't truly exist."

"She'll not want to speak with me at the moment."

"Because you hurt her."

"Because she thought I wanted her to be my mistress."

"Good Lord."

"I'm assuming that was a prayer?" he retorted, using her earlier words against her.

"It was certainly a prayer for your hopeless soul. Divine intervention is necessary if this is what you call wooing."

"It was a misunderstanding."

"Clearly, because I seem to remember you saying you'd not shame her by even asking such a thing… yet if it were a misunderstanding. Why the tears?"

"I, er, well."

"Good Lord."

"You are becoming quite pagan in your use of the Lord's name this day."

"I'm praying. Believe me, you need it. You didn't explain yourself did you?"

"I was quite offended that she'd think so low of me—"

"Because your reputation is all sweetness and light, is that correct? Did you ever consider that she *knows* all about you? Your reputation that is?"

"I assumed yet didn't think... oh."

"Oh." Lady Southridge mimicked.

Charles glared.

"You need to make this right."

"Your power to state the obvious is astounding. I'm quite breathless with mysteries you'll unravel with your next words."

"Don't mock me. I'm your only hope."

"Save me."

"Believe me, your blackened soul is going through its share of penance with what you'll be needing to undertake to win this girl."

"How do you know that?" Charles bit back.

"Think—"

A knock sounded at the door, immediately arresting Charles' attention. For a moment his heart stopped as he thought it just *might* be Carlotta, but the very thought mocked him. Why would she want to talk with him after his last performance?

"Enter," Charles called, his tone authoritative. The need to feel in control of something, even as small as someone's entrance, was overwhelming after the uncertainty of the past few moments with Lady Southridge.

The door didn't open.

"Enter," Charles called louder, but he shared a curious glance with Lady Southridge who simply shrugged.

When no one entered, he strode to the door and opened it himself.

"Hello, your grace." Berty curtsied prettily and batted her dark eyelashes at him.

"Er, hello, Berty." He stumbled. "What brings you... here?"

"I live here, your grace."

"Yes, I'm quite aware of that."

"Then why did you—"

"Why are you knocking on my study door?"

"Oh, well I was hoping to say hello to you, since you haven't seen us yet." She beamed at him, one tooth missing from her top row and making her smile almost comical.

"Well, hello, Berty."

"Hello, your grace."

Charles wiped his hand down his face. This conversation was going in circles.

Tight circles.

Berty didn't seem concerned however; she continued to beam at him.

"Berty!" Carlotta's voice carried down the hall as she strode towards them, her eyes fixed on her young charge. But Charles noticed a becoming blush to her cheeks that wasn't there a few seconds ago.

"Miss Lottie." Berty turned and curtseyed, all sweetness and light as if she were not about to get a scolding.

Charles had to hand it to her for being so brave.

Or foolish.

At the moment, he wasn't in the frame of mind to decide.

Not when his focus kept straying to the lightly pursed lips of Miss Lottie. They were no longer bee stung from his earlier kisses, but their color, the color of his favorite pink roses in his mother's rose garden, captivated him, stealing all rational thought.

"Berty, you are to be studying with your sisters in the school room. You did not have my permission to leave. And we've spoken about his grace's need for privacy.

"I *did* give him privacy. I didn't even go into his study. It's not allowed and I obeyed. I just waited in the hall." Berty shrugged.

Carlotta closed her eyes, her exasperation evident. "Be

that as it may, you still did not have my permission to leave."

Berty sagged her shoulders and nodded. "Yes, Miss Lottie."

"Please excuse us, your grace." Carlotta spoke without looking at him.

Who knew that the lack of a glance could hurt worse than the worst glare?

Chapter Ten

Carlotta refused to look at him. No good would come from that; all it would do was remind her of his lips, the touch of his hands at the small of her back, the heat from his body as it pressed up against hers while he stole her breath with his kisses.

Yes, it would be a very bad idea indeed.

No, no, no, no...

She glanced up. Betrayed by her own body, her traitorous eyes glanced up at him and immediately her heart shuddered at the blatant heat in his expression.

Heat she knew all too well.

She was still feeling the burn from earlier.

Turning to Berty, she said, "Bid his grace good day, Berty."

"Good day." Berty curtseyed, again, then beamed at him, offering the duke a smile that revealed almost all of her little teeth, at least the ones she had not lost recently.

Then it struck her.

Her teeth.

Berty had been so delighted when she finally lost her

baby teeth and the fact that she lost the one in front, absolutely overjoyed her. Her sisters teased her that she looked like a pirate, and Berty had basked in their story spinning over the idea.

Berty was still beaming at the duke.

He was staring at her as if he were trying to understand why.

Carlotta's heart pinched as she felt pity on him for being so out of his element, so she went against her own self-preservation and reached out an olive branch.

She moved slightly so that she was behind Berty, then glancing up she waited till she got the duke's attention. Quickly, she smiled and pointed to her teeth.

The duke's brow furrowed for a moment then his countenance lit up, understanding clearly dawning his in mind.

Carlotta held her breath as he bent down to Berty's level.

"Well, Miss Berty. It seems as if something is amiss. As beautiful as your smile is, it seems to be missing... something." He gave her a serious expression as he made a show of studying her teeth.

Carlotta bit her lip to keep her grin in check. Her heart softened, it was times like these when he didn't even realize how compassionate and kind he was, that it unsettled her the most. It gave her a glimpse into what could never be hers.

Which hurt more than she was willing to admit.

"Do you think, your grace, that I look like an evil pirate?" Berty asked, leaning forward.

"Er, well, I suppose." He glanced up to Carlotta as if to discern how to answer such a question.

She shrugged.

"I'd have to say yes, you do put me in the mind of a pirate, though perhaps, not an evil one."

Berty swished her skirts as she swayed. "Thank you, your grace. I better obey Miss Lottie now. Oh! Welcome to

Greenford Waters!" She reached out and hugged his neck and then released him abruptly and began skipping down the hall.

The duke had such a look of shock on his face that Carlotta couldn't contain her bark of laughter. Immediately covering her mouth, it wasn't quick enough to stave off the bubbling mirth.

The duke stood, offering her a raised eyebrow before she was able to contain herself.

"I say, Charles, what is going on out here?" Lady Southridge walked into the hall, her gaze immediately settling on Carlotta. With a beaming smile, she nudged the duke in the back, her gaze shifting expectantly to him before returning to Carlotta.

"Oh, yes." The duke cleared his throat and made the introductions. "Lady Southridge? May I introduce you to Miss Carlotta, governess to my three wards."

Carlotta inwardly winced at the stoic introduction. It was for the best, she knew, but that didn't stop it from hurting.

But if he wanted her to be his mistress, he had another thing coming. It was best this way.

It had to be.

"Miss Carlotta! I'm so pleased to meet you! I've heard so much about you!" Lady Southridge gushed, her green eyes warm and inviting, not at all cool and calculating as Carlotta had anticipated.

"It's a pleasure to make your acquaintance." She curtseyed and took a small step back, feeling as if she should further distinguish between their ranks in society.

"You're every bit as lovely as Charles said." Lady Southridge stepped forward.

Carlotta cut a startled glance to the duke who seemed to be very uncomfortable.

She understood his discomfort completely. It mirrored her own emotions.

But she didn't feel the least bit sorry for him.

"I'm sure his grace was simply being very kind," she demurred, rapidly searching for a way to escape, one that wouldn't offend the duke's guest.

"Oh Charles isn't one—"

"Miss Lottie was helping locate a wayward young lady, who is now, presumably, back in the school room. I'm sure you're anxious to attend to her." The duke offered her the perfect escape.

She nodded and bid her farewells, walking down the hall. Her emotions were a jumbled mix of gratitude and heartache. Gratitude for the duke giving her the perfect escape from an awkward situation, but heartache for the way it was done.

Cursing her oversensitivity, she almost didn't hear Lady Southridge's scolding. "Well, if *that* is how you treat her, no wonder you're having issues. I am now fully convinced you need my assistance."

"Bloody—"

"Charles!"

"Hell."

Carlotta couldn't help but smile as she walked the rest of the way to the schoolroom. She puzzled over the meaning of Lady Southridge's words, but more than anything, she delighted in someone telling the great Duke of Clairmont what to do.

It was about time.

****

Later on that afternoon, Tibbs came in to request their presence at dinner. The girls squealed with delight over having a formal dinner rather than their usual quiet meal in the nursery. Noticing the girls' attention severely lacking, Carlotta quit lessons earlier than usual to allow the girls ample time to ready themselves.

Carlotta helped them dress and enlisted the help of Mary, the maid, to help arrange their hair. By the time Tibbs came into escort them to dinner, Carlotta had scarcely arrived in the nursery, having rushed through readying herself. She chose a deep green gown, one that was simple enough for a governess, but that highlighted the color of her eyes. She went a step further and loosened the prim chignon at the base of her neck so that it was more of flowing style that softened her features.

More than once she told herself she was taking these steps for herself, not the duke, and that she would have done the same if he was not in residence and instead was having a practice formal dinner with the girls.

But her heart called her mind a liar.

While she would have dressed the same, even done her hair in a similar manner for the practice dinner, the idea wasn't the same. She wanted to look beautiful, and if she were honest, she wanted him to *want* her. Even if nothing could come from it, she simply wanted to be wanted. Shaking her head at her own folly, she followed behind Tibbs to the parlor where they were to wait till dinner was served.

Lady Southridge was already waiting. She was a beautiful vision in fine velvet of a deep green that appeared every bit as expensive as it surely was. Her eyes lit up as the girls entered, surprising Carlotta with the warmth in her gaze as she stood and approached the girls.

"My! How lovely you all look tonight! I'm so glad we can have you for our guests!" she gushed. Bethanny blushed and curtsied. "You must be... Bethanny, correct?" Lady Southridge inquired with a smile.

"Yes, my lady." She demurred perfectly.

"And you are Beatrix?" she asked.

"Yes, M'um." Beatrix curtsied as well, her face blooming with color.

"I'm Berty! Don't forget me!" Berty rushed up, gave a precariously deep curtsey, and then beamed up, showing off, again, her lost tooth.

"Oh! It seems that you have lost a tooth! My! You are becoming quite a young lady, aren't you?" Lady Southridge bent down slightly and caressed Berty's face in a decidedly motherly fashion.

Carlotta was conflicted. The duke had said that she was more of a maternal figure to him... but was that accurate? Was Lady Southridge's opinion differing? She surely acted as if she belonged at Greenford Waters, and was taking a marked interest in his wards. Carlotta felt a surge of jealousy she quickly stomped out.

It wasn't her business.

And if the duke married a woman who would care for the girls, all the better. She refused to give any voice to the raging emotions in her heart, and turned to offer her own warm greetings to Lady Southridge. "How are you this evening, Lady Southridge?"

"Very well! I do love it here. My husband has an estate not too far away, but I do find that Greenford Waters is more to my own personal taste," she commented, her eyes bright and clear.

Carlotta tried to puzzle piece this information together.

And was failing miserably.

"I'm sure you're quite welcome here." Carlotta spoke, trying to maintain her composure in her deep confusion. Thankfully, Lady Southridge turned her attention to Bethanny, questioning her about her age and talking about the London Season.

Carlotta lost herself momentarily in her thoughts even as she kept half an ear on their conversation between the two women. If Lady Southridge was married... then she wouldn't be pursuing the duke. Carlotta felt a huge burden of relief, but a dark foreboding nipped at the heels of such a release.

What if she were his mistress?

It wasn't unheard of. In fact, it was quite common for

those women of quality who had produced an heir and spare to take their pleasure elsewhere than their husband's bed.

Suddenly, it all made sense.

No wonder the duke was so cold and harsh when she mentioned a mistress.

He already had one.

But why present her as a parental figure? It still made no sense.

At that moment, the very man in her thoughts entered the room. His presence filled it, permeating the very air with the power of his person. He scanned the room and when his gaze met hers, she felt the connection like a physical caress. An unwelcome shiver of delight tickled her back and she forced her gaze away. Though she was now watching Berty, she continued to *feel* his gaze upon her.

"Charles, of course now you show up! Leave it to you to arrive just before we're called to dine. You really must set a better example," Lady Southridge chided, her face still lit up in grin.

Her manner towards the duke was even more confusing.

"Lady Southridge, accept my deepest apologies. Allow me to make amends by escorting you to dine."

Carlotta glanced back to him, assuming he would be looking at Lady Southridge as he spoke to her.

But he wasn't.

No, he was still gazing intently at Carlotta.

Swallowing compulsively, she glanced down once again.

"If you don't mind Charles, I would rather be less informal this evening. The girls and I have much to discuss and I'd prefer to keep their company rather than yours. Goodness knows how tedious you can be." She spoke in a teasing manner.

"Heaven forbid I should subject you to my objectionably tedious manners," he replied dryly.

"Lovely. Now girls, shall we make our way to the dining

room? Now, I'm sure your lovely governess has told you this before, but usually the highest-ranking gentleman will escort the highest-ranking lady to supper. But since we're dining informal, I'm breaching proper conduct." She leaned down to fake whisper, "Please keep my indiscretion between yourselves." She raised an eyebrow till the girls, giggling behind their gloved hands, nodded their obedience.

Carlotta lifted her own hand to cover her wide smile at the antics of Lady Southridge. The woman was a confusing mystery, but regardless, Carlotta found herself rather liking the unconventional woman.

Lady Southridge started towards the door. "Do not forget your manners Charles, escort the young lady." She nodded in Carlotta's direction and left. The girls following close behind. Bethanny paused at the door, glancing back at Carlotta and giving her a wide smile.

A *knowing* smile.

Immediately heat burst into her cheeks, surely causing a deep blush.

"I'm under firm orders to escort you to the dining room." The duke bowed crispy before her, then extended his arm.

"Thank you," she replied. Keeping herself firmly in check, she allowed him to lead the way, but she refused to *feel* anything.

Her arm tried to make her feel her how warm he was, even through the material of his fine coat.

Her nose tried to overwhelm her with the spicy peppermint scent of him.

Her eyes tried to remind her of his strong jaw, his full lips and the broadness of his shoulders.

She silenced each sense that tried to be overwhelmed with *him*.

"Quiet again?" he inquired, his tone light but distant.

It pulled her away from the lockdown she had forced upon her senses.

"Simply nothing to say, your grace," she responded.

"Again, I find that hard to believe. But perhaps I'm not asking the right questions. What do you think of Lady Southridge?"

"She is very kind to the girls, for which I'm very grateful. She seems genuinely interested in them."

"I assure you, she is."

"That is good to hear."

The silence continued for a second longer.

"How are the girls doing in the studies?" he asked as he reached up to adjust his collar.

"They are very intelligent young ladies and quick studies in all I place before them," she answered.

"That is good to hear." He used her same words, which was not missed by her. A smile tipped the edge of her mouth at the oddity of their conversations. Truly, if they weren't arguing, they were kissing. If they weren't kissing, they were arguing. This was quite possibly the first calm conversation they had carried and it was also the most boring, mundane—"

"What has caused that mischievous grin to delight your face?" He stopped their progress and turned towards her, his eyes taking in her features in a decidedly passionate manner that was in conflict with the lightness of his question.

"My thoughts are my own." She shrugged, attempting to walk towards the dining hall once more.

His hand closed over his arm, trapping her hand and halting her progress.

"Now I find that my interest is overwhelmed. Please share your secrets, Miss Lottie." He raised an eyebrow, but a smile tipped his lips causing his expression to be quite mischievous.

"As I said, your grace, my thoughts are my own. There is no requirement for me to share them as they belong to me only," she responded lightly, but her grin widened.

"Then I shall try to tease them from you."

"That would be a very bad idea."

"Haven't you realized that I'm quite fond of that which pertains to bad ideas, lack of thinking and all things impulsive?" he teased, alluding to their earlier conversation.

Carlotta sobered as she reflected on that same conversation, rather, the end of it.

"Yes. I'm quite aware. It's to your benefit that I'm opposing in nature and find myself more inclined to be less impulsive and more thoughtful. They'll be waiting, your grace." Carlotta kept her tone light, but her gaze surely conveyed her desire for the topic of conversation to come to a close.

The duke paused, searching her gaze before his expression became distant.

"As you wish." He began to lead towards the dining room once more. As they were rounding the corner, he paused. Before Carlotta could question what he was about, he leaned in and kissed her, softly, sweetly. It was nothing more than a quick taste of her lips before he withdrew, leaving her not even moment to return the kiss.

Which she wouldn't have done, or so she told herself.

Immediately he began their way towards the dining room once more

"Before you say anything…" he began in a soft whisper, like a caress. "I did that because I had to. As much as it is impulsive, without thought to propriety and lacking all judgment on my and your part, I find that kissing you is simply like breathing. Absolutely necessary. Hang everything else." He gave her a penetratingly endearing gaze just before they entered the dining room.

Carlotta, feeling quite overwhelmed with the whole situation and his declaration, was thankfully guided to her chair and sat. She glanced up to see the three girls staring at her openly, questions written all across their faces. But to their credit, they didn't speak. Although Bethanny was struggling mightily to conceal her amusement.

When she turned to Lady Southridge, she noticed a twinkle in the lady's eye, one that was deeply amused and impish. Both traits she wouldn't have earlier associated with the finely turned out lady.

Clearing his throat, the duke sat and dinner began.

Carlotta had never been so thankful for the distraction of soup in her life.

"Tell me about yourself, Miss Carlotta." Lady Southridge began as she delicately sipped her soup.

Apparently, soup was only a distraction for *her*.

"There isn't much to say, my lady," Carlotta replied, hoping to keep the conversation dull enough to allow for a change in subject. So far, the duke hadn't ever asked about her background, but she assumed he knew through Mr. Burrows or even Mrs. Pott. Being forced into service because of one's poverty wasn't a discussion Carlotta's remaining pride was willing to explore, regardless.

"Oh, come now. I'm sure there's something to share! Where did you grow up?" Lady Southridge persisted.

"Not too far from Bath," she answered vaguely.

"Is that so?" Lady Southridge's eyebrows rose.

"Indeed." Carlotta nodded then returned to her soup, not offering any more information.

"So have you been to Bath before then?"

Carlotta swallowed her warm soup slowly, procrastinating so that she wouldn't have to answer Lady Southridge's question till absolutely necessary.

Pride was a wicked beast.

"Yes, on several occasions," she answered politely. Though her answers were not lengthy, the last thing she wanted to do was offend the duke's guest.

"Miss Lottie knew all about the Crescent and the Abby! We had a picnic at the park and everything!" Berty exclaimed, her face lighting up with the joy of adding to the adults' conversation.

"Did she now? You girls are very lucky to have such a learned governess." Lady Southridge gushed to Berty then turned her adoring gaze to the older girls. "Tell me, what else did Miss Carlotta tell you about Bath?"

"Well…" Beatrix turned a questioning gaze to Carlotta, as if to ask if they were allowed to divulge any information. Carlotta smiled sweetly, there was really nothing else she could do.

"She showed us the shops on the bridge, it was quite amazing. I've never seen a bridge like that."

"Ah yes! I remember that as well. What park did you picnic at?"

"I believe it was Sydney Park," Bethanny answered.

"We fed the ducks! Do you like to feed ducks Lady Southridge?" Berty asked her face lit up in an endearing smile.

"You know, it has been an age since I've fed the ducks. Perhaps, if it is permissible with his grace, we could venture out tomorrow and do just that."

"Oh! Can we your grace?" Berty wasted not a moment to plead her case.

"I believe that will be acceptable. I'll have cook prepare you a picnic for your excursion. I, however, will remain at the estate. There are several issues on the estate I must address."

"Has something happened?" Lady Southridge asked, her tone slightly fearful."

"Why, no. Just normal upkeep." The duke allayed her concern.

"Oh, then if it is not pressing, why can you not accompany us?" Lady Southridge wiped her mouth with the linen napkin and gazed directly at him.

Carlotta could have sworn she saw him squirm.

That is, if dukes actually *can* squirm.

"I have not been to this estate for quite a few months, I have a responsibility."

"Come, Charles," Lady Southridge commanded, but her tone was light.

Carlotta decided that she wouldn't want to be on the bad side of Lady Southridge. She was quite… assertive.

"After all, your wards will want to spend time with you." She cast a sweet smile to the girls, who upon seeing her gesture slightly with her hand, the one that was out of the duke's line of sight, they nodded enthusiastically and smiled.

"See! They want you to attend! Surely you can postpone your business till later that afternoon," she chided.

"Very well. I'll attend you." His tone was reluctant and he cast a wary glance towards Carlotta.

Which of course, she didn't miss.

And because she was already contemplating the complexities of their non-existent relationship —really there was no other word to describe a kiss between a duke and governess!— she decided that she had to control her emotions better and there could not, under any circumstances, ever — ever, ever— be any more kisses.

It was entirely to confusing,

And she was not going to fall for a man who would leave her ruined.

Because that was the only logical outcome.

After all, dukes did *not* marry governesses.

Either way, at least she would not have to attend their outing tomorrow, as it was her one day off for the week. She doubted the girls remembered, especially since she hadn't taken a day off since they arrived. There was nothing for her to do unless she wanted to go to Garden Gate, and as much as she missed her home, she didn't want to revisit the memories that haunted the halls.

"Miss Carlotta, would ten o'clock be an acceptable time for you and the girls to take your leave?" Lady Southridge asked.

So much for keeping her plans silent.

"Actually, my lady, tomorrow is my day off. The girls will be ready for you by that time, however." She spoke as politely as possible.

"Oh, dear," Lady Southridge commented, her expression crestfallen. "I suppose I did not consider that." She took a deep breath. "I know you have no reason to amend your plans, especially for me, but I would consider it a great personal favor if you would go with us tomorrow. I'm not as familiar with Bath and your expertise would be most welcome."

Carlotta considered her words. "I wouldn't want to intrude… and seeing as his grace will be attending you, he is likely far more wise to the architecture and layout of Bath than I, my lady."

Lady Southridge glanced to Charles and cleared her throat. Twice.

When the duke didn't look up from his soup, she turned back to Carlotta.

If it wasn't so awkward, she would have laughed or at least smiled.

"I'm afraid his grace, by his own admission, not been here for some time. I'd much rather have someone more familiar."

It was a far stretch. Bath was one of the oldest cities in England and not much had changed to its infrastructure. Carlotta knew that, she suspected that Lady Southridge knew that as well. But she couldn't rightly challenge the lady's word. So with a resigned nod, she accepted. "I'd be delighted then, Lady Southridge."

"Perfect! And I'm sure his grace will see fit to give you a separate day off for your leisure," she gushed.

The duke glanced up, his face wincing as Lady Southridge shifted slightly.

If she didn't know better, she would have believed that the duke had been kicked under the table by a very pointed slipper belonging to Lady Southridge.

Good thing she knew better.

She smiled regardless, however.

"Yes, yes. Perhaps the day after tomorrow? Will Friday be acceptable?"

"Indeed, thank you, your grace."

"Yes, well..."

The conversation continued to ebb and flow through the several-course dinner. Carlotta was thrilled to watch her charges use perfect table manners, correct posture, and engage in polite conversation. To see a tangible reward for her efforts quickly outweighed the embarrassing conversation earlier.

As dinner finished, the duke excused himself, only to be called back by Lady Southridge. "Charles? Would you please escort Carlotta to the parlor? I would love to walk with the girls once more and I find that I'm in need of entertainment. Do any of you beautiful young ladies play the pianoforte?" She turned her attention to the three girls.

"Yes, m'um." Bethanny and Beatrix nodded.

"I'm learning, Lady Southridge."

"That is wonderful. I'd love to hear you all play! It's settled. Charles? What room holds your delightful instrument?"

"That would be the green room. If you'll follow me," he responded graciously.

Carlotta stood and waited for the girls.

"Oh, do carry on without us. I find I need to finish my wine. I'll be just a moment. The girls will direct me, won't you?" Lady Southridge turned to the girls.

"Of course," Bethanny responded. Then, as if she questioned whether to continue or stop, "I'm sure we'll be only a moment. Lady Southridge wished to tell me more of the London Season and we'll simply continue that conversation when we rejoin you."

Carlotta narrowed her eyes slightly. Lady Southridge was beaming, Bethanny simply looked *too* innocent and Berty had a very confused expression on her face.

"But you weren't talking about London, you were trying to—"

"Berty! I, er, need your help," Beatrix cut in, her eyes frantically casting about for something that would make her statement true.

"Oh? What happened?" Berty asked, distracted.

"It seems it is just you and I," a soft voice spoke from behind her. A chuckle escaped and warmed her insides at the rich sound. "Let them have their secrets, Miss Lottie. Truly, what is the worst that can happen?" he asked.

"You have no idea what you're saying." Carlotta turned towards him, prepared to give him a very exasperated expression, but he was much closer than she had expected.

Much, much closer.

Her breath caught as she almost walked into his chest. The scent of cedar and peppermint immediately enveloped her and caused her determined thoughts to grow foggy.

"Shall we?" he asked, his voice for her alone.

She nodded, not willing to trust the strength of her voice.

He reached out and placed her gloved hand on his arm, then led them into the hall amidst whispers that trailed behind them.

She must remember to tell the girls about the difference between the classes. This was one area they were not to meddle with.

"Surely being alone with me isn't too trying?" he asked, his gaze intent on her face.

"Trying isn't the word I'd use."

"Oh, what word then? Charming? Handsomely distracting? Witty, intelligent—"

"My, however am I to choose with such a diverse list of options?" she replied wryly.

"Honesty is always preferable to flattery."

"Says the duke," she mumbled.

"Indeed, however I'm curious as to why you said it."

"So are you looking forward to tomorrow's picnic?" Carlotta tried to change the subject. She had no desire to explain herself for the slip.

"Yes and no. You are not sufficiently distracting from my previous question. However, just in case my dashing countenance stole your train of thought—"

"Are you always so humble?"

"Yes, and the question was, why does it matter if a duke preferred honestly to flattery? I find I'm quite curious as to your answer, Miss Lottie."

Carlotta sighed. "If you must know, as duke, you undoubtedly are surrounded with people who wish to flatter you as a way to obtain your good graces. That lends the idea of you surrounding yourself with honesty, quite challenging, your grace."

"Charles."

"Pardon?" Carlotta stopped mid stride.

"My name is Charles. You are free to use it, when we are alone of course."

"No, thank you, your grace."

"I fully intend on calling you Carlotta so I felt it necessary to be fair."

"I'd prefer you not address me so familiar, your grace."

"Carlotta…" He paused, his eyebrows raised in challenge at his use of her Christian name. "Forgive me for being so forward but as a woman I have kissed, thoroughly, and on many occasions I might add, my use of your Christian name is far less scandalous than the previous."

Carlotta took in a deep breath. "I believe I've stated my opinion on the kisses, your grace. To allow you to use my Christian name would simply undermine my previous statement."

"Ah, yes, the no kissing. Seems to be working rather well, wouldn't you say?" he teased just as he leaned down and pressed a quick kiss to her shocked lips.

"Your grace!"

"Charles," he amended.

"You cannot simply... kiss people."

"I don't. I kissed, *you*."

"I'm a person and I don't wish to be kissed!"

"Yes, you do. You just are afraid."

"Yes, no. I mean—" She broke off, sighing heavily and releasing his arm. "Yes, I'm afraid, for obvious reasons we have *already* discussed. I'm not one to trifle with. I have more... respect for myself than that. I ask for you to exhibit that same... respect towards me... please." Her tone was pleading. In all truth, she was powerless to stop him if he did continue to kiss her. Not only was he stronger, but she had no *desire* to stop him either. She wanted his kisses, but her heart had a quite different view than her mind. And her mind won the logical debate. It had to end.

Now.

"I swear to you that I'm not simply dallying with you, Carlotta."

"Your grace, you cannot do anything but. I'm simply a governess. Nothing more... but nothing less either. When I left London, you explained that whatever attraction we felt must be denied, that was why you were sending us away. Why then, are you here now? I'll not say I'm not attracted to you. I am. As much as it terrifies me, I am. But there is nothing that can come of it. So please. I ask, no, I beg of you. Please. Allow me to remain respectable in my own eyes and do not kiss me or try me further. I fear my own will is not strong enough against the force of your own.

Carlotta gazed at him, her heart angry at the unfairness of the situation. How miserable that the longing, the heat in their kisses could never be explored further unless it accompanied a fall from grace.

Life, as always, was never fair.

And Carlotta was quite aware of that fact.

But never so much as right now.

"You're resolved?"

"Yes."

"And what if I don't agree?"

"Then you'll be going against my wishes, and in that, reacting in a selfish manner that further explains your intentions towards me." She held her breath, hoping she didn't offend him by challenging his honor.

But there was no other way.

"Very well."

A stony silence followed them to the room with the pianoforte. Once the duke opened the door and led her in, he bid her goodnight and left abruptly. A few moments later the girls and Lady Southridge arrived, giggling and smiling. When they noticed the duke's absence, Carlotta answered their questioning gazes before they could speak.

"His grace retired early."

Lady Southridge's brow drew together and she glanced to the door. She took a small step as if debating whether she should drag him from his chambers, but Berty chose that moment to begin to play her latest piece on the pianoforte, stealing Lady Southridge's attention.

The girls all took turns, playing perfectly and singing together. As soon as it was acceptable, Carlotta ushered them to bed.

As she lay on her own pillow not much later, she reminded herself that it was for the best.

No matter how wonderful his kisses were, they would only serve to destroy her.

After all, Eve's sin was to taste the forbidden fruit.

And there was nothing more forbidden to a governess than her employer.

Chapter Eleven

The next day dawned clear and bright. Carlotta helped the girls ready themselves after breakfast and soon they were waiting in the parlor for the carriage to be brought about. The girls seemed nervous. Carlotta watched them carefully and tried to reassure them with a hand to their cheek or a slight squeeze to their shoulder.

As the time for their departure arrived, Lady Southridge came into the room, her nose red and her eyes watery. "Oh my dears! I cannot believe it! All our travels and today of all days I am to catch a cold! I tried all morning to relieve myself of this miserable—" She coughed delicately into a handkerchief. "But is of no use! How I wish I could go! But you must enjoy your time without me." She gave a trembling smile.

Then sneezed.

"How miserable, Lady Southridge." Carlotta felt pity for the poor woman. There was never anything as miserable as being sick.

Except for maybe pining for a duke she could never have.

Yes, being sick was second to that.

"You go on without me," she said again. As if on cue,

Bethanny strode forward and wrapped her arms around Lady Southridge's shoulders. "I'll stay with you, that way you'll have some company."

"Yes, me too," Beatrix said quietly, going to stay beside her sister.

Berty bit her lip, glancing to Carlotta then to Lady Southridge, she seemed to debate her options.

"Berty..." Bethanny spoke lowly, warning.

"Oh all right. I'll stay too." She pouted and walked over to the rest of her sisters.

"There's no reason for me to go then—"

"No! I insist! You must attend Charles, he'll be ever so lonely."

"I'm sure his grace—"

"Needs you," Lady Southridge completed, her voice suspiciously strong.

As if realizing, she coughed. Twice.

"But—"

"Ah! Here is Tibbs, I'm assuming the carriage is ready?" she asked.

"Indeed."

"Please escort Miss Carlotta to the carriage. Is his grace waiting?"

"Indeed. Miss Carlotta."

Carlotta tried to protest, but found herself all but pushed into the hall by Lady Southridge who promptly closed the parlor door and left her standing quite dazed with Tibbs.

"Surely I should—"

"Attend his grace," Tibbs completed. It seemed as if no one wanted her to complete her own thoughts any more.

Or make her own decisions seeming as she soon found herself sitting with the duke in the open carriage on their way to Bath.

Alone.

Actually, a driver and two footmen, but it *felt* alone.

To alleviate her own tension, she nodded to the duke then turned to stare at the scenery.

"Where, might I ask, are the rest of our party?" the duke asked as they made their way down the lane towards Bath.

"Pardon?" Carlotta turned her gaze towards him.

"The girls, Lady Southridge? Why are they not attending us?" he asked mockingly.

"You weren't aware?"

"Apparently not."

"Lady Southridge came down with something and was terribly ill." Carlotta explained.

"Hm. And the wards?"

Carlotta felt her eyes narrow. However, knowing he said that simply to spite her, she chose not to rise to his bait.

"They elected to stay with her. They seem quite attached to her."

"Or simply overwhelmed and obedient."

"Excuse me?"

"Lady Southridge is far from sick, I assure you. Disease doesn't dare interfere with her plans. Illness itself shakes in fear of that woman. I've never seen her sick a day in my life. It's unlikely she started now."

"She appeared quite ill."

"Odd, I saw her earlier and there seemed to be nothing amiss."

"Oh."

"Yes, indeed. Oh."

"What do… that is… why would she—"

"Because she is of the mind that you are the very woman to save my blackened soul from my previous life of a wastrel."

"Oh."

"I believe you said that already."

"Indeed."

"We've used that one too. For a governess you're surprisingly narrow-minded on your use of vocabulary."

"I'll disregard your insult in light of the situation."

"How noble of you, *Miss* Carlotta." He nodded as he said her name, as if communicating his effort to respect her wishes.

She smiled a thank you.

"Why would Lady Southridge consider me your salvation?" she asked, immediately regretting the question. All it would do was open the conversation she had so neatly closed the night before. "Forget I asked that."

"If that is what you wish."

"It is."

They continued on in silence for a few minutes. Carlotta tried to think of intelligent conversation but kept drawing a blank.

"Tell me, how far away is your home from Bath?"

"It's a morning's ride by carriage."

"I see. Did you travel there often?"

"Depending on the season."

"Must you always answer so succinctly? Can you not elaborate in the slightest?"

"To what end? That part of my life is no longer."

"Be that as it may, it was still apart of you at some point. And because of that, has contributed to the woman you are today."

"The contribution you mention is obsolete."

"Your tone smacks of bitterness, Miss Carlotta. What are you not telling me?"

"Forgive me, I'm not bitter. Truly. It's somewhat difficult, being close to where my home once was, only to have it be my home no longer," she answered honestly, repentant at her short tone earlier.

"That would indeed be difficult." He paused. "So tell me your favorite sights in Bath."

They carried on that conversation in various veins throughout their quick tour of Bath till they ended up in Sydney Park. The duke's hand was warm as it covered hers, helping her alight from the carriage. The thrill of his touch was a pleasure she allowed herself to enjoy for only a moment before she released his grip. They strode to the river's edge and watched the languid water flow softly.

"We shouldn't tarry long. Your guest will be wondering about us." It was a pathetic excuse but she was desperate. At this point, she felt her resolve to keep distance between them crumbling.

"Without eating? Your ladylike appetite might be able to withstand our journey back, but mine will not!" he teased, his clear eyes crinkling around the edges with humor.

"Then far be it from me to cause you to suffer," Carlotta teased as she began to lay out their meal.

"My stomach thanks you."

Carlotta couldn't resist a saucy smile at his banter and handed him a bright red apple.

"Ah, the forbidden fruit," he commented lightly.

"Pardon?" Carlotta felt her good humor drain. Hadn't she called *him* that just last night as she pondered on her bed?

"The forbidden fruit. I suppose we don't know if it was truly an apple that Eve ate when tempted by the serpent, but the same truth still applies." He remarked as he rolled the apple between his palms before taking a bite.

"And what truth is that?" Carlotta asked.

"That we are doomed to always want what we cannot have." His eyes were dark, his full lips drawn into a firm line.

"Indeed."

"Is this where you took the girls?" he asked as they finished their meal. Standing he helped her up as well.

"Yes. You should have seen their delighted faces when I gave them bread crumbs to feed the ducks."

"They enjoyed themselves?"

"Immensely."

"I wouldn't suppose you had any extra bread crumbs on hand?" he asked, his blue eyes dancing with mischief.

"I do." She opened up a hamper that a footman had deposited behind them and pulled out a tied linen cloth. "Here." She opened it and handed a chunk of stale bread to the duke. His warm fingers caressed her palm as he took it, his darkening gaze communicating that the contact was more than intentional.

Carlotta dropped her gaze.

"Stale bread is quite a delicacy for ducks, is it not?" he teased, his countenance brightening with charm.

"They are quite assertive, aren't' they?" she commented with a laugh as a duck thumped another of its companions with its wing in efforts to steal an unusually large chunk of bread.

"They simply know what they want," the duke commented lightly.

Carlotta glanced from the ducks to him.

His expression was anything but light. Rather it was smoldering with double meaning. Her heart caught in her throat as she felt her lips tingle with the memory of his kiss.

As if sensing her weakening he took a step forward, then paused, his expression a myriad of conflict. Carlotta broke their gaze and turned to open the hamper once more to deposit the now empty linen.

"We should return," she commented lightly and stood not paying attention to her whereabouts. Her waist was warmed by his hand as he pulled her back against his chest. His breath was warm as it caressed her neck, his lips inviting as they placed a lingering and heated kiss just below her ear.

"Your grace, any one could see—"

"Let them."

"But—"

"Carlotta, you talk entirely too much," he said lightly as he traced up her arm with his other hand, leaving delightfully warm tingles. Slowly he turned her around. Unable to meet his gaze, she stared at his perfectly tied cravat, swallowing her own desire.

"Carlotta," he whispered, petitioning her.

It was her undoing.

Slowly lifting her gaze, she visually caressed his strong jaw, the soft sensual curve of his lip, the straight arch of his nose until she finally lost herself in the blue regard that burned like the hottest part of a flame.

He leaned in to kiss her, but paused as if warring against himself. No doubt, he was considering her words from last night.

To kiss her would prove his selfish intentions. Or so she said. Right now though, it would be more of a selfish action to not kiss her.

Never had she wanted anything so desperately.

Forbidden fruit.

Before she could restrain herself, she rose upon tiptoes and kissed him. It was delicious; he tasted like apples and smelled like spice.

His passion consumed her.

Yet all she could think about was how this was her goodbye kiss. All the other kisses, it had more or less taken. Not this one. This one was of her own accord.

Tragically, it was also meant to be goodbye.

He deepened the exchange, and Carlotta felt her control slipping to the precipice of the edge of her own desire. Abruptly she pulled back, not knowing she was so close to the edge of the river. She wobbled on her heel, waving her hands wildly to gain her balance.

It was no use.

She fell, with a mighty splash, into the river.

"Carlotta!" the duke shouted, reaching in and pulling her out.

Her dress clung to her, the water chilly and immediately causing her to shiver. He fussed over her like a mother hen and draped his coat over her, in spite of her claim that such a foolish action would ruin the coat.

"Better to ruin the coat than cause you to catch a fever," he remarked, firmly.

The open carriage was chilly and Carlotta shivered the whole way back. He seemed to debate what to do. Finally, with quite hesitant movements, he slipped over to her side of the carriage and reached for her hand. With a question in his gaze, he paused to make sure she wouldn't refuse him.

After a moment of indecision, she decided that any warmth would be welcome, and reached out to meet his grasp half way. His gaze warmed, like slowly melting honey. The heat from his hand traveled up her arm and into her chest, making the urge to shiver lessen. But even with the connection of their hands, the earlier amusement and lighthearted banter was now stilted. *We are forever doomed to want what we cannot have.* The duke's statement haunted her, taunted her, and reminded her of just how true it was. To his credit, the duke tried to pull her into conversation, and while her responses were polite, she felt herself withdrawing into her own shell for protection.

When they arrived back, the girls spilled out of the house to greet them, stopping short when they saw her shivering and dripping, wearing the duke's coat.

Lady Southridge followed behind the girls, appearing quite miraculously recovered. She eyed Carlotta questioningly.

"Did you enjoy yourselves?" Bethanny asked, her eyes darting from her to the duke.

"Did you feed the ducks?" Berty asked.

"How was your trip?" Lady Southridge asked, her eyes dancing with... hope?

"Yes, Lady Southridge, and yes, Berty we did feed the ducks, and yes, Bethanny," Carlotta responded.

"And you can all ask your questions once Miss Lottie is dry, now, off with you all!" Charles barked impatiently and, because apparently she wasn't moving fast enough for him, she found herself swept up into his arms and being carried, quite quickly into the warmth of Greenford Waters.

"Tibbs!" he shouted for the butler, who had only just stepped from around the corner.

And was now wincing from the loud bellow from the duke.

"Please have a bath readied for Miss Lottie, there was a… mishap and we do not want her catching a chill."

"Very good, your grace." He bowed and left.

"I can walk," she ground out. The warmth of his hands seemed to engulf her, penetrating the chill and igniting a fire that she would have rather ignored.

"No, you can't," he replied stubbornly

"I—"

"No, you can't."

"Do you always simply tell people what to do, or am I the only fortunate one?" She turned to narrow her eyes at him.

"I—do not have to answer that." He gave her but a slight glance before he turned down the hall towards her room.

"I see my point is made." She raised an eyebrow.

"Most women would be thankful I was seeing to their welfare," he responded impatiently.

"I'm not most women."

He paused mid-stride and gazed at her with piercing intensity. "Believe me, Miss Lottie, that is a truth I'm far from missing. Now…" He paused, glancing to her lips then visibly forcing himself to meet her gaze once more. "I promise to release you once you are to your room, but allow me the honor of getting you there quickly, and without further interruption."

She paused, wanting to argue, but seeing that it was for some unknown reason, important to him to act so needlessly chivalrous, nodded instead.

As they reached her room, he set her down gently, his

hands slightly caressing her legs as he set her upright. "Thank you for your company today." He reached out and grasped her hand; lifting it slowly he let his penetrating gaze caress her face till he placed a very long, lingering, and delightful kiss to her hand.

"You're welcome."

With a very polite bow, he backed away, his dark gaze intent and anything *but* polite.

And before she could give into the impulse and smolder of his gaze, she rushed to the safety of her room.

****

Charles walked back towards the entrance and was quickly intercepted by Lady Southridge.

"So?" Lady Southridge questioned, her eyes wide with excitement.

"So… what?" Charles questioned. The girls had fallen into step behind Lady Southridge, who was following him and well, he felt quite like a mother duck with four little impatient ducklings nipping at his heels.

Rather, he felt like the bread crumb they were all chasing after.

"Come now, Charles, surely you figured out how to use this perfectly orchestrated situation to woo her."

"Lady Southridge!" He turned and eyed the young girls meaningfully.

"Oh, they knew all about it. They helped. Didn't you girls?" she asked, beaming with pride.

"Helped?" Charles choked on the word.

"Yes your grace," Beatrix nodded soberly.

"I'm quite… speechless."

"A first I'm sure. Now, since we gave you such a perfect opportunity, please tell me you didn't waste it."

"If you want me to woo the lady, you'll have to inform

her as she has no desire for me to woo her," Charles said, his tone slightly bitter.

"Of course she wants you to woo her! And if she doesn't then you, sir, aren't doing it correctly."

"I didn't know I was in the audience of such master at wooing," he retorted dryly.

"She does want you to pursue her. She's just scared," Bethanny said softly, as if reluctant to enter the conversation.

"Why would she be scared?" he asked, though he suspected he knew the answer all too well.

"You're quite handsome, your wealthy, titled, and have a reputation as dark as sin," Lady Southridge remarked. "Forget you heard that last part girls," she added, spearing them with a withering gaze.

They nodded quickly.

"I don't think that's why she's reluctant," he remarked.

"Oh, then why? It's not as if you've been completely dishonorable. You took the opportunity and said your intentions today, did you? I mean, that would be the logical road to take," Lady Southridge said.

"My intentions?" Charles questioned.

"Yes you're…" She paused. "Girls, can you please occupy yourselves? I'm going to require some privacy to converse with his grace."

"Yes, m'um." They scattered.

Charles wished he could go with them.

"Now, if I'm understanding this correctly, you had a perfectly beautiful day with a perfectly wonderful lady who, I might add, is an impoverished baron's daughter who is currently employed as your governess—"

"I'm quite aware of who she is, madam."

"Forgive me if I question your ability to connect simple and logical thoughts. Did I misunderstand that you find yourself in love with this girl?"

"Yes, I mean no. Yes I'm in love with her, bloody sorry I

am but it's true."

"A more romantic declaration I've never heard," Lady Southridge responded sarcastically. "No wonder the poor girl ran to her room." She huffed indignantly.

"Now see here."

"No, you see here! You didn't tell her your intentions were honorable? You didn't declare yourself? I gave you the perfect opportunity on a platter and you disregard it!" She all but shouted, exasperated.

"Forgive me if I resent constantly being rejected!" he shouted back.

"You're only being rejected because she thinks you're wanting her as a mistress or dalliance! Your reputation isn't exactly pristine, Charles. You fell in love with a smart woman. That is a draw back when she can logically take your reputation and deduct what you're intention could be! You have to tell her otherwise!"

"I—I—"

"Did not?" Lady Southridge finished.

"No."

"You are an idiot."

"Thank you," he replied.

"What are you going to do about it?" she asked. The woman was worse than a dog with a bone.

"I'm not sure! I can't simply buy her a necklace or trinket of some sort. As proper as she is, she'd never accept it. She'd probably just be offended thinking I was trying to buy her off."

"Which is exactly what you *would* be trying to do," Lady Southridge shot back.

"Mistresses are so much easier to handle than potential wives," he mumbled.

"They last longer."

"Touché."

"So I ask you, what are you going to do?"

"According to you, I'm going to tell her my intentions."

"Good boy.

"I'm not your lapdog.

"Your right, my lapdog is quicker to catch on than you, my dear boy."

"Now, tell me how exactly did you fall into the river? That is one fiasco I did not expect."

"I'd rather not talk about it."

"I never once thought you would. My question stands, regardless."

"You are the most meddling—"

"I'm helping. Admit it. You wouldn't have had the whole afternoon alone if it weren't for me. In fact…" She began to circle him, much like a hawk teasing its prey. "I'm the only reason you're even *here*."

She had a point.

Damn it.

"That doesn't give you license to interfere," Charles grumbled.

"How did—"

"She fell."

"I gathered that since I assumed you didn't push her for sport," she replied wryly.

"I'd push *you* in for sport."

"How providential that I was not in attendance."

"She… stepped back and fell in."

Lady Southridge just stared, waiting, clearly not concerned with how long it took for the truth to come out.

"I kissed her, she ran and fell. Happy now?"

"Not particularly."

"Nor am I."

"How often do you do that?" she asked after a brief pause, her eyes narrowing slightly as if contemplating the meaning of life.

"Do what?"

"Kiss her."

"More than I should."

"And how often do you simply talk."

"Talk?"

"Yes, conversation. Even you aren't that much of a lack wit, Charles. I shouldn't have to spell it out for you."

"We talk."

"Not enough."

"How would you know?"

"Because I *know* you, Charles. And, as much as it pains me to say and risk inflating your ego further, if she spoke with you, if you charmed her like I know you're capable of, then she would be running to you, not away."

"I'm quite sure she'd run away, besides I'm quite trapped as it is. I doubt there's much I can do."

"Why so hopeless?"

"Because *this* conversation has been so positive?"

"No… er…" She had the good grace to look slightly humbled. "But what do you mean?"

"Last night she asked for me to leave her alone, to no longer kiss her. And she said if I did, then I'd be simply showing my own selfish nature… implying that my intentions are only selfish and disregarding to her own convictions. So you see, my hands are tied. I kissed her today, she backed away but before… before she did I could *taste* her…" He paused as if considering whether to continue, he was so caught up in his thoughts it almost said too much.

"I'm not a prude, you tasted…?"

"Her desire… her attraction. She wanted me, but she doesn't *want* me. I don't understand it. It's so bloody confusing."

"Compromise her."

"Excuse me?" Charles felt his jaw drop and his eyes blink in shock.

"Compromise her."

"No."

"Why ever not? It would solve so many of your issues and you'd have to marry her."

"Yes... but... It's not what she wants."

"Ah."

"Ah?"

"So you're more concerned about her than yourself?"

"Of course."

"Then you are truly in love. Show her this side of yourself Charles."

"You just said for me to be charming, to win her not bare my bloody soul."

"Forget what I said. Bare your soul, Charles. Then thank me later." She smiled genuinely and excused herself, leaving Charles spinning with disbelief.

****

"Foolish, foolish, foolish." Carlotta continued to chide herself over and over for her weakening that afternoon. Thankfully, she was given a tray for her meal and didn't need to face the duke. She paced the floor while losing herself in her thoughts.

The truth was that she wanted him, more than anything she'd ever wanted in her whole life. *Forbidden fruit.* Never had there been a more accurate description for the duke.

As the night wore on, she became more and more restless. Her emotions kept her mind spinning, refusing to allow a moment of relaxation let alone sleep. It was almost midnight when she grew exasperated enough to trek outside her room and borrow a book from the library.

Anything that would get her mind off his smile.

The glow of his gaze.

His *taste*.

She walked soundlessly down the hall, a few flickering

candles lit the path she already knew quite well. She reached the door and opened it slowly, lest it make any noise and alert someone of her whereabouts.

The last thing she wanted was to be caught in her nightgown and robe. But, anticipating a quick return, she didn't bother to dress simply to borrow a book.

A low fire burned in the grate, offering orange light to the grand library. Ceiling-high bookshelves were carved out of the walls, offering a myriad of tempting distractions for her overwrought mind. She padded softly to the corner where she knew to find poetry. Something metered, preferably rhyming that would lull her to sleep. She pulled out an especially thick volume with a red spine when she heard the door open. Gasping she drew herself back into a corner, hoping the darkness would shield her.

And because fate wasn't kind, the duke walked in, in nothing but his breeches and thin white shirt.

He looked alike a wealthy pirate. His usually combed hair was tousled like he had been fighting sleep just as furiously as she. The soft light didn't illuminate his features well, but cast shadows across his face giving him a darker, more dangerous appearance.

Her heart raced.

Her lips tingled.

Her breathing increased till she could smell him— cedar and smoke. Peppermint and something so dangerously alluring it made her knees feel weak.

He didn't see her, or else didn't act as if he had. As he made his way to the fire, she noticed his shoulders sagged slightly, as if bearing a burden too heavy to bear. He sighed, a bone-weary exhale that sounded full of sorrow, and her heart constricted with sympathy. Her arms ached to hold him, to encourage him to share his burden with her.

The fire crackled loudly, sending a fury of sparks in the air. Carlotta jumped, startled by the eruption when her attention had been so arrested by the duke.

He turned.

His eyes widened, his shoulders straightened and his eyes, now illuminated by his close proximity to the fire, burned gold.

Her mouth went dry.

"Carlotta." He spoke. Not questioning, simply stating her name.

"Your grace."

He nodded slightly then turned back to the fire.

"You should go." He spoke quietly, not in the usual commanding tone she was accustomed to hearing. He closed his eyes as if in pain.

"Are... are you well, your grace? Is there something I might help you with?" she asked tentatively, stepping forward. Forgotten was her lack of proper attire, all she could think of was the burden in his expression. A burden she wished to relieve him of.

"Y—no, I thank you for your offer but I believe under the circumstances you should go. Preferably running down the hall and locking the door behind you. I would not want to do something, as I did earlier today, that would go against your wishes. I... admire you deeply but my self-control has distinct limits. His tone was soft, raw.

"I see." He was abiding by everything she asked.

Then why did she feel so... empty?

It was the wise thing to do, to heed his advice. His self-control wasn't the only one that had limits. She started towards the door, placed her hand on the cool knob and paused. Glancing over her shoulder, she watched him stare into the fire.

"Go, Carlotta."

She twisted the knob.

Opened the door, and watched his eyes close as if pained. She closed the door, the loud clicking of the mechanism echoing in the room. The duke, his eyes still closed, leaned forward, his head resting on the stone hearth. Reaching his arms out, he braced himself against the wall. His shoulders, usually covered in his coat, ripped beneath his thin shirt, impossibly broad. His tousled hair combined with the golden hue of the fire gave him the appearance of a pagan god chiseled from bronze. He pushed back from the wall, his muscles tightening with the motion and he turned.

His gaze was unguarded for a split second before it hardened into a steely self-control she hadn't expected. "I thought you left. You *should* leave."

"No." She surprised herself.

And apparently, him, for his eyes widened.

"Carlotta—"

"What burdens you so?" she asked, risking a few steps toward him. Drawn in by his gaze, she felt deliciously captive.

A ghost of a smile teased his lips. "Forbidden fruit," he answered plainly.

"It would seem that is quite an epidemic tonight." She tilted her head, offering him a small smile, even as her heart thundered from the startling truth of her own admission.

"Truly?" he asked, his normally light eyes dangerously dark.

"Is that all that troubles you, your grace?" she asked, avoiding his question.

He opened his mouth as if to question her, then paused. Twisting his lips slightly, he continued. "Just because it was a short answer doesn't mean it isn't a lengthy plight, Carlotta."

"Oh."

"And unless you want to find me kissing you with a decided lack of restraint, I suggest you take pity on me and leave." He took a step back. "Please."

It was the 'please' that melted all of her remaining resistance. With a small step forward, she held her breath, knowing that she was changing everything but unwilling to consider the consequences.

He took another step back.

She took another step forward, a smile playing at her lips.

"I'm at a loss as to what about this situation is comical, Carlotta," he whispered darkly.

"Well, your grace, it seems to me that *I* should be the one running from you, not the other way around. If you don't stand still I'll find myself hopelessly insecure about your possible rejection," she teased.

She stepped forward.

He closed the distance with three rapid steps and, sliding his hand around her back, pulled her into a fiercely passionate kiss. There was no gentle tutoring, no easing into the bliss of his affection. It was a vortex, a standing still to immediately sprinting type of kiss where there was no awareness of anything but the other person. He pressed into her, rubbing her back with a demanding touch and his other hand stole under her robe and caressed her hip. Carlotta gasped at the thousands of pleasurable sensations that coursed through her at his touch. Never had she experienced such… desire. It should have scared her, but it felt so… right.

His lips left hers, trailing down her jaw, nipping, tasting and devouring her tender flesh till he rained kisses down her neck, stopping at a particularly sensitive spot just below her ear.

"Please tell me you're real, that I'm not dreaming this fantasy," he whispered in her ear before nipping the lobe.

"Not… dreaming." Carlotta gasped.

He groaned and swept her up into his arms, captivating her lips once more. Carlotta's body felt on fire, everywhere he touched. She wanted more, something deeper, more intimate but she had no idea what exactly.

But she knew she shouldn't want it as badly as she did at that moment.

He laid her on the chaise and covered her with his body,

pressing into her and giving his hands free reign to caress her arms, hips, the line of her shoulders, the soft fabric covering her belly. She gasped as he reached higher till the smallest sound brought to the forefront all of the consequences of their actions.

The door opened.

Lady Southridge gasped.

Charles swore.

And Carlotta wished the settee would envelop her, saving her from the premature demise of humiliation surely taking place.

Unable to move with the duke still quite on top of her, she wiggled till she gained her freedom. Lady Southridge's mouth was open in a silent 'O' before she spun on her heel and left, closing the door firmly behind her.

"That wasn't expected," the duke commented dryly, as if the world hadn't completely shifted off its axis.

"Er, no?" Carlotta commented, not sure what to say, or how to interpret his casual meaning.

He stood, offering his hand out towards her. She accepted and smoothed out her nightgown, her extremely wrinkled, very crumbled nightgown.

Hot shame washed through her.

Breathe in, breathe out.

Anything to keep the tears inside, anything to keep whatever shreds of dignity she still possessed.

Who was she kidding?

Her dignity was gone... just like her pride.

Closing her eyes she refused to look up into his face, not sure or wanting to know what was written in his gaze. Hadn't she told him earlier she'd not be his mistress? That she was not a light skirt? She had just proven herself a liar, and everything she had just refuted.

"Carlotta," he murmured.

Tears burned. How could something that *felt* so right now

feel so… wrong?

"Look at me, love," he tipped her chin up with his finger.

She opened her eyes, allowing the tears trapped within to spill out onto her cheeks.

"Tears? No, there shouldn't be any tears. I know you're giving yourself quite the scolding, but it's not necessary. I'll make a respectable woman out of you yet, my prim little governess." He smiled endearingly, enchantingly and for a moment, she allowed herself to pretend.

To pretend that she *was* the princess. That miracles did happen and that renowned rakes could be redeemed for the right woman, for the hope of true love.

But as soon as she indulged in the fantasy, her mind was flooded with the truth. If he married her, he'd be laughed at, maybe not to his face, but behind his back. *Brought down by a governess.* She could hear the gossip, feel the sneers in her direction and the cutting remarks to her back. London would be scandalized and he'd lose the respect his title demanded.

The quality do not fraternize with the help.

Her father's words echoed through her heart, causing it to crack, crumbling in defeat and love unrequited.

Because it *may* have been different if he loved her.

Even just a little bit.

But attraction and lust were not love.

His soft tone interrupted her thoughts. "…It will simply take a few days to obtain a special license. Lady Southridge will be the soul of discretion, I assure you, and your reputation will remain pristine, your virtue quite intact." He traced her face with soft fingertips, wiping her tears away.

Because she did the *wrong* thing, he now was doing the *right* thing. And it was costing him. She didn't doubt his attraction to her, she didn't doubt that he had strong emotional attachment, but she did doubt her ability to keep him. He was, after all, a duke. If that weren't enough, the rumors of his mistresses and dalliances were the stuff of legends. *Bad* legends, but legends nonetheless. How could she hope to hold his affections for more than a few months, years even? He'd tie himself to her legally, but his heart? Who would own that? The thought of him keeping it to himself, or worse yet, giving it to another when she was the one sharing his name was enough to cause a nauseous feeling to overwhelm all other senses. No.

She'd save them both. She'd save her heart and at the same time, save his dignity. He'd thank her later when he married some rich titled woman with all the right connections. Surely, he'd forget about her, even if she never forgot about him.

"Carlotta?" he asked, his tone like a caress.

She shivered in desire.

"Yes?" she asked, her plans solidifying.

"What do you say?" he asked.

"I think it would be best to speak of it in the morning, your grace." She glanced down to the floor.

"Carlotta—"

"Please…" And because she knew it would provide enough of a distraction, she used his name. "…Charles."

His gaze ignited and he bent down to kiss her once more, lingering long enough for Carlotta to force herself away, against her own fierce desire to melt into him once more.

"Good night," she whispered, forcing herself to walk to the door.

"Carlotta, are you sure… please wait," he pleaded, holding his hand slightly out towards her.

"I just need time… please."

He watched her intently, she could see the war within his mind battling in the dark and intense gaze, but he nodded.

Sighing silently in relief, she made her way into the hall… and ran.

"Please, Carlotta, Miss Lottie, stop. I beg you." Lady Southridge's voice called to her just as she reached her door.

"Forgive me, my lady. My behavior was inexcusable." Carlotta paused with her hand on the door, willing to escape as soon as possible, but her conscience —the blasted morality that decided to wake up *after* the fiasco in the library!— wouldn't let her escape to the safety of her room till she apologized.

"No, no there's no need. I'm afraid it's rather my fault," Lady Southridge commented guiltily.

Carlotta turned, watching the fair woman take a few tentative steps towards her.

"You see, I was, am, quite a meddlesome person. Charles, Lord knows I love him like my own son, but he is quite... dense. I, er, suggested earlier that he compromise you, never once considering he'd actually take my advice—"

"Lady Southridge there's no need—"

"Please, let me explain. You see, Charles, he is quite in love with you, my dear. I'm sure that's why he acted as he did."

"By compromising me?" Carlotta asked, toneless. Though her memory reminded her that she was quite responsible for said compromising.

"By trying not to. I assume your virtue is still intact?"

From the top of her head to the tip of her toes, she flushed, blushing painfully. Nodding she stared at the ground, willing it to open up and swallow her.

"Your innocent nature will not understand just how much restraint he was using to keep you that pure, my dear. Rather than see his actions as dishonorable, please consider the opposite. That's all I wanted to say, and I feel I'm failing miserably, but please, that fact that he *didn't* truly compromise you is the truth of the depth of his love. Because he thought of you, before the demands of his own."

With a nod, Lady Southridge disappeared into the night.

Carlotta blinked in the darkness, her mind spinning, trying to digest all the information from Lady Southridge. It was an intriguing thought to consider the converse of his actions, especially when coupled with her responsibility in the whole disaster.

Intriguing and damning, because if there ever was an appropriate time for a lady to curse, it was now.

Damning because more than ever she realized just how it was all her fault.

****

Carlotta awoke to a soft knocking on the door. Expecting Berty having suffered a nightmare, she opened the door without putting on her robe.

Tibbs, not Berty was on the other side of the door, the austere butler, averting his eyes rapidly once he saw her, cleared his throat before speaking. "Miss Carlotta, you have a caller. Forgive me for the early interruption, but your solicitor, Mr. Burrows is quite adamant that he sees you, immediately." He spoke articulately, to the floor.

"Thank you, I'll be down in a moment once I'm, presentable."

"Very good, he is waiting in the green parlor."

"Thank you."

Carlotta closed the door and leaned against it, her heart beating rapidly. For a split second, when she opened the door and, glancing down to see Berty, saw a highly shined pair of boots, she thought it might have been the duke. Her heart raced, relieved and simultaneously disappointed when she saw it was in fact, Tibbs, rather than the duke in the hall.

What could Mr. Burrows possibly need? Immediately her heart seized in her chest. *Garden Gate*! Was there something amiss? Her mind began to conjure up thousands of miserable plights from fire to locusts destroying her last connection to her family. With reckless speed, she put on the simplest frock and pinned her hair into a barely respectable bun before all but racing to the parlor.

"Mr. Burrows?" she asked, tilting her head and walking into the sitting room.

Smiling, he stood and strode over to her, bowing politely and gesturing for her to sit.

If he was smiling, surely he had good news, didn't he?

"Forgive my early arrival. You've been a difficult woman to track down. I would have been here last night but my arrival in the area was too late to call. I stayed overnight in Bath and didn't want to waste another moment in relaying to you the change in your situation."

"Change?" Carlotta asked as the small framed man sat across from her and withdrew a stack of papers from his bag.

"Yes, indeed. I have not only discovered that your investment in the Caribbean has turned an immense profit, but, that you have a cousin, a wealthy viscount who upon learning your familial relationship, wishes to marry into your family so that Garden Gate will not fall out of the family." He nodded as if utterly satisfied.

Carlotta blinked A profit? A way to keep Garden Gate? Could it be true?

"I don't know what to say, your grace," she whispered, not trusting her voice. Thoughts of the duke, his laugh, the twinkle in his loch blue eyes and the taste of his kiss flooded her mind.

"I'm sure this is all quite a shock. I'll explain further if you'd like, but I'm hoping you'll accompany me to Garden Gate. There are a few documents you'll need to sign, and I've taken the liberty in having the Viscount Darby meet us there. His reputation is valiant, I might add. I took the additional liberty of making sure he wasn't a fortune hunter or wastrel."

"Thank you," she mumbled, because there was nothing more to say.

"Of course! Will you accompany me? I'm sure, given the change in your station, the duke will excuse you for a few days. In the meantime I'm sure he'll be able to find a replacement governess for the wards."

The girls!

Carlotta took in a sharp breath. The girls, she couldn't leave them for any length of time without saying goodbye.

"If the duke allows me, I'll leave with you as soon as I can pack. I must say goodbye to the girls, however. And I must return in a few days' time, I'll not shirk my responsibility, regardless of my change in station." She didn't mention that she didn't know how she'd be able to say goodbye to the girls, or the duke. Nor did she even entertain the idea of marrying the Viscount Darby. It was too much, the fresh emotions from last night had left her heart raw.

Thought the idea of marrying the Viscount did offer the perfect escape. But she refused to dwell on it. One moment at a time, that was how she'd survive the day.

"Let me find Tibbs." Carlotta stood and walked to the door. After locating the butler, who was standing down the hall as if waiting for her, she explained the situation, omitting the part about the Viscount. Tibbs nodded sagely.

"Miss Lottie, his grace is unavailable. He left earlier this morning, at dawn. I'm not sure when he will return either as he didn't give me any particulars. However, if memory serves correctly, this is your day off, having been rescheduled from the previous day because of your picnic. Am I correct?"

"Er, yes, actually. Thank you Tibbs. That will work out nicely. I'll simply leave his grace a note explaining my plans."

"Very good. Should we expect you back tonight?"

"Actually, no. I will likely be gone for a few days. That *will* not work. Hmm." Biting her lip, she thought over a solution.

"If I may be so bold, Miss Lottie? Perhaps you can speak with Lady Southridge?"

"Yes, I believe I will. Do you know where I might find her?"

"In the dining room, breaking her fast."

"Thank you, Tibbs. Please excuse me."

Her heart beat rapidly as she approached the dining room. In all truth, the last thing she wanted was to talk with Lady Southridge after their midnight conversation, but there was no other option with the duke gone to who knows where.

And, upon reflection, she wondered quite painfully where he *had* gone. In the whirlwind of all the information from Mr. Burrows, she hadn't stopped to consider the duke's absence. Why had he left? He couldn't have returned to London, his guest, Lady Southridge was still in attendance.

Carlotta had to hold off on her runaway thoughts as she entered the dining room only to find Lady Southridge absent, the girls, however, were all grinning at her through slightly sleepy eyes.

"Good morning, Miss Lottie!" Bethanny chirped, her expression beautiful if not slightly drowsy.

"Good morning, girls. I trust you slept well?" Carlotta asked as she rounded the table and caressed Berty's cheek, smoothed Beatrix's hair and squeezed Bethanny's shoulder in succession.

"Yes, quite well," Beatrix spoke softly, the shiest of the three sisters.

"I'm thankful to hear it. Have you by chance seen Lady Southridge?"

"No, the dining room was empty when we arrived. I haven't seen her all morning," Bethanny answered, her expression curious.

"Oh, I need to speak with her."

"Is something the matter?" Berty asked.

"Yes, no, well, I'm going to be gone for a few days." Carlotta sat down across from the girls, wanting to be as honest as possible. They deserved as much. "It would seem that an investment my father made, who I can now tell you, was a baron, has made a change in my financial position—"

"You're going to not be our governess anymore?" Beatrix burst out, her expression horrorstricken.

"What?" Berty shouted, tears brimming in her eyes.

"Yes, I'm still your governess. I'm not saying *that* kind of goodbye, I'm just needed to address some matters."

"Oh, you'll be back though?" Bethanny asked her eyes wide with concern.

"Yes. I'll be back."

The girls visibly relaxed at her reaffirmation. "I do need to find Lady Southridge, however. I'll come and say goodbye before I finally depart."

"Very well." The girls spoke hesitatingly, their eyes wary despite her reassurance.

Carlotta quit the room and began to search for Lady Southridge.

And found her speaking with Mr. Burrows.

Never had she been so thankful for client confidentiality.

"Lady Southridge." Carlotta curtseyed. "I have a matter to discuss with you, if you have a moment?"

"Of course." Lady Southridge eyed Mr. Burrows worriedly and turned to Carlotta.

"It would seem that an investment my late father made in the Caribbean, has changed my situation. Mr. Burrows wishes for me to accompany him to my estate, Garden Gate, to finalize the particulars. To do this, I'll be needing a few days off from my responsibilities."

"I see." Lady Southridge appeared worried.

"I'll be returning, my lady." Carlotta felt compelled to add.

"Oh, I'm sure, I meant I never mean to imply that you'd disregard—" She eyed Mr. Burrows. "—the girls." She cleared her throat, and shot a very direct gaze to Carlotta.

Because she didn't mean the girls as much as she meant the duke.

She was not to disregard *the duke*.

"I wouldn't disappoint the girls in such a way." Carlotta glanced to the ground, not able to meet her implication with the affirmation she sought.

"You *will* return." Lady Southridge spoke in a clear authoritative voice,

"Yes, my lady."

"And I'm assuming you're asking my permission since his grace is strangely absent?"

"Yes."

"Very well. I'll expect you to be back within three days' time, however."

"Very good, Lady Southridge. I'm sure I'll be back by then, if not before."

Lady Southridge took a deep breath, her eyes narrowing slightly before she turned and excused herself form Mr. Burrows and Carlotta.

"If you'll excuse me, Mr. Burrows, I'll gather my things."

Nodding he strode to the fire and waited.

****

Less than an hour later Carlotta sought out the girls. After whispering goodbyes amidst hugs and far more tears than she cared to admit, she walked down the hall to where Mr. Burrows waited.

"It is clear you've grown quite fond of your charges," Mr. Burrows commented, his eyes compassionate.

"I have, indeed." Carlotta sniffed delicately.

"Garden Gate is not far. With such a maternal instinct, I hope I'm not being to forward in stating that perhaps you should seriously consider the Viscount's offer of marriage. Surely a woman such as yourself with a remarkably tender disposition should have children of her own." He led them down the stairs.

His words hit their mark, but not in the way he likely

would have assumed. Carlotta immediately imagined little fat babies... with summer sky blue eyes and thick patches of dark hair, wide lips and mischievous grins remarkably like their father's.

The very children she could never bear.

But ached for regardless.

"I'm not offended, Mr. Burrows. Thank you for your kind insight," she responded.

"I hired a maid from Bath, she'll attend you in case there isn't one available at Garden Gate. I hope that's acceptable?"

He helped Carlotta into the carriage then entered as well. "Thank you, I hadn't considered that."

"You're a very wealthy young lady, the daughter of a baron. Your station requires far more propriety than that of a governess." He shrugged.

Immediately they set towards Garden Gate, a war waging within Carlotta. Not three months ago, she was lamenting leaving her precious home, certain her heart would remain in the halls of Garden Gate without her. Yet, now, the further she traveled from Greenford Waters, the fainter her heartbeat sounded to her own ears.

Her heart had found a new home. And while she struggled to convince herself that it was because of her fierce attachment to the girls... she knew the truth. No matter how she fought it, tried to forget it and insisted against it, her heart was held by none other than the Duke of Clairmont.

The very man whom she could never have.

Chapter Twelve

"Lady Southridge! Damn it all where are you?" Charles shouted from the hall, his tone menacing and impatient.

"Charles what is the matter and why, in heaven's name, are you bellowing?" Lady Southridge emerged from the library, her expression irritated.

"You! The only thing preventing me from strangling your meddlesome neck is the fact that you have information I need, and if I killed you, I'd never know it. I ask you, where. Is. Carlotta?" He spoke through clenched teeth. He felt like a wild animal barely under control.

That morning he had left at first light to ride and obtain a special license. It had taken him longer than he anticipated due to a miserable rainstorm that halted his progress on the way home. Expecting to sweep Carlotta away at the first opportunity he was shocked, and quite crushed to realize that the very woman he was intending to sweep away, was not in residence.

Betrayal, hurt and anger all fought for dominion in his heart… until he found a target— Lady Southridge. Poor Tibbs had wisely taken a few steps back from the duke when he explained the situation. And who had granted the permission for her to leave.

Truly, he had never been more tempted to commit murder in his life. What had those daft women been thinking? He had been very clear about his intentions with Carlotta. And why in the bloody hell did Lady Southridge let her go?

"Carlotta will be back in a few days, Charles. Settle down. You look positively wild. Absence does make the heart grow fonder, you know."

Not the thing to say.

He took a very deliberate step towards her, unblinking he stared hard into her eyes. "I dare you to repeat that."

Lady Southridge took a step back.

Perhaps the woman had some sense after all.

"Charles, she was with her solicitor, Mr. Burrows. Didn't Tibbs tell you? I'm assuming you know that much since he said I had given her permission." She glanced up as if exasperated.

She had no idea what exasperated truly felt like.

"Yes, I heard about the bloody investment making a bloody return and giving her back her bloody financial independence and her going to settle everything at her bloody estate. What I want to know is why you couldn't have her wait for me? I was obtaining a *special license*... Am I making myself quite clear?"

"I—I wasn't aware you had an understanding."

"Yes, well..."

"When I spoke with her last night she didn't imply..." She trailed off as if catching herself. Her eyes widened.

"You did *what?* When? When did you speak to her?" Charles took another step forward.

"I—I, well, I felt responsible."

"In what way could you have possibly shouldered any blamed for—" He began to roll his eyes.

"I told you to compromise her."

"Dear Lord." He felt his face drain of blood. "You didn't..." He couldn't even think of a damning enough swear word to describe the wretchedness of the situation.

"I—er... well I said that I felt responsible because I didn't think you'd actually *do it,* and I said that since she left with her virtue intact, she should consider how much self-control you were exhibiting... oh bother... it sounds quite miserable when I re-tell it. But I swear it was quite eloquent last night."

"Bloody brilliant damning hell."

"That was quite a list."

"It's not remotely long enough." He wiped his face with his hands. "This is a disaster. I have no words. I... I don't even know what to say." He walked away. Of all the wretched things! No wonder she ran away as soon as possible! Hell, *he'd* have ran away from himself if the tables were turned.

"But if you have an understanding, I mean you are engaged, aren't you?" Lady Southridge was wringing her hands, trying to grasp at straws that would make the bleak and miserable situation somehow have a silver lining,

There was no silver lining.

Black. The horizon was black.

Especially since he actually never *asked* her... simply *told* her that they'd marry.

"You're not answering," Lady Southridge whispered.

"No. I'm not." Charles stared straight ahead, seeing nothing.

"There's no understanding, is there?" Lady Southridge whispered even softer.

"I'm not sure. I rather told her about my plans to obtain a special license rather than ask for her hand."

"But... you said you loved her... right?"

"No."

"What *did* you do?" Lady Southridge's voice rose in volume. Charles turned towards her and saw her hands firmly on her hips, her lips in a grim line.

"I kissed her quite senseless." He was seriously wondering if it could get worse.

"Men!" Lady Southridge threw her hands up in the air and walked a few steps away, then paused.

"Berty, dear, this isn't the time," she spoke softly to the young girl, her tone kind.

"Your grace, I heard something and Bethanny said I should tell you."

"Oh, what did you hear, Berty?" Charles tried to calm himself and pay attention to the little sprite of a girl.

"I followed Miss Lottie, but she didn't see me. Just as her and that wretched man who took her away were about to walk outside, he said... well... it sounded like a viscount was meeting them at her home, to marry her." Berty glanced down, her eyes brimming with tears. "She'll never come back, will she, your grace?" Berty burst into a sob, throwing herself at Lady Southridge's legs and burying her face in her skirts.

"There, there child. I'm sure she'll be back. She never said anything to me—"

"Why in the hell *would* she tell you?" Charles spoke darkly. Of course, things could get worse, why had he even asked?

"Because, I don't know. I—Berty? Did you happen to hear the viscount's name?" Lady Southridge asked as she smoothed her hair away from her cherub-like face.

"Banby? Darby? Something like that," Berty replied, her words muffled by the skirts.

"Darby?" he asked. Recalling the man associated with the title, Charles felt his blood run cold. Darby was from an old titled family, had more than enough wealth, a sterling reputation and was all around respectable. The blasted man was even decent to look at, or so he was told. In all truth, he was perfect for Carlotta.

More honestly, he was everything that Charles was not, at least in the character department. Oh, he knew he had enough wealth and his title alone would recommend him, but character? He was severely lacking, that and self-control, and the ability to ask the woman he loved to marry him.

Yes, that sin was at the top of his list right now.

"Thank you, Berty. Can you please tell your sisters I'd like to speak with them?" Berty glanced up with shining eyes.

"Yes, Lady Southridge." She scampered off to find her sisters and Charles watched her, his soul completely hopeless.

Just last night he was on top of the world, he didn't even sleep but left at first light to secure a special license so that he could marry her before she had a chance to escape.

Apparently, she had a chance to escape and took it.

"This is an unforeseen road block." Lady Southridge tapped her chin.

"Road block? This is a bloody massacre."

"It's not as if she's married Darby already."

"But she should."

"What?"

"She should. He'd be perfect for her."

"But—"

"But I'm not... perfect for her. I can't even remember to say I love you when it's needed most. I fail at simple communication."

"But you feel it?"

"Like Zeus' lightning bolts every time I see her."

"Then why give up?"

"I—"

"Your grace?" Bethanny asked, her soft voice tentative as she approached with her sisters.

"Yes, Bethanny." He sighed, numb.

She glanced to her sister, Beatrix, then turned back to him, her eyes wide. "You have to go after her, your grace. I... I think she might be in danger."

"Danger?" Charles echoed; he fought between fear and disbelief. Mr. Burrows was anything but dangerous. "How so?"

"She was quite distressed, she was... crying."

"Crying?" he asked, his eyes widening."

"Yes." Bethanny nodded vigorously. "She was sobbing really, and that man, Mr. Burrows? He said something about her being too attached to us and... I'm not sure but it looked like he forced her into the carriage."

"He did *what?*" Charles felt his blood boil. Could it be? Was there perhaps hope?

"So you see, you simply *have* to go after her, your grace. What if something horrible happens?" Bethanny was waving her hands about, her eyes wide with fear.

"Lady Southridge, you say here at Greenford Waters. If Car—Miss Lottie returns before I do, keep her here. Am I understood?" He leveled his most stern gaze at the woman.

"Yes, we'll tie her up if need be."

"I doubt that will be necessary... but if it is, do it," Charles amended.

"Tibbs! Get over here man!" he bellowed down the hall. Tibbs rushed forward. "I need my horse ready immediately!" he shouted to the frenzied butler.

"Yes, your grace." Tibbs bowed then ran.

Ran.

"Charles, you don't know where Garden Gate is!" Lady Southridge called after him as he rushed down the hall.

"No, but I can ask. Surely, someone in Bath will know. I'll ask Lord Whipple's wife, she knows everyone around these parts."

"Very well, please... send word as soon as you know something."

"If I'm able. Now, excuse me."

Rushing to his room, his valet helped him dress in fresh riding breeches and a warmer coat. Losing patience with his slow pace, he ran to the stables and mounted his chestnut stallion that had just been readied and was waiting. The magnificent beast pawed the earth, anxious to be off.

Charles understood the feeling.

Moments later, he was thundering down the lane towards Bath, praying that Lady Whipple was in residence and accepting visitors. He was a desperate man and was not above resorting to desperate measures. But in the interest of time, it would be far more expedient if she simply told him the information he needed to know.

Less than two hours later, he was following the route given by Lady Whipple's butler to the estate of Garden Gate. It was far closer than he anticipated, only a two-hour ride from Bath. By his account, he had only an hour left of travel, which was providential since the sun was beginning to set lower in the western sky. As his horse galloped towards his destination, Charles gave his mind its freedom as well.

A thousand different scenarios flashed through his head as he considered why Mr. Burrows had forced Carlotta's departure from Greenford Waters.

Was there a sinister side to Lord Darby? One that was hidden? Was Mr. Burrows using her for his own treacherous purposes? Charles felt that scenario quite unlikely, he had known the solicitor for many years, but just how well *did* he know him? Well enough to trust him? With his money and affairs, yes, with Carlotta? No. Truth was, he wouldn't trust anyone with Carlotta.

Including himself.

But he was in love with her; that had to make up for his multiple sins in lacking to communicate that affection.

At least he hoped.

By the time he saw the modest estate in the distance, he had worked himself into a lather, both physically and mentally. Without hesitation, he dismounted as his horse skidded to a halt just before the front steps. Taking the stairs three at a time, he didn't knock, but opened the door and strode in. His heels were loud on the tile floor, but he didn't care. Let them know he was coming, let them quake in fear and wonder just what avenging force was coming for them.

He heard voices and turned towards the sound, stopping short when he saw Carlotta, smiling.

Laughing really.

What hurt worse was that her smile which filled his veins with fire, and that laugh that stirred his very soul… felt silent as soon as she saw him.

And for the first time since riding out to rescue her, he entertained the miserable thought that perhaps, she didn't need him after all.

Maybe he just needed her.

Maybe he was the one in need of rescuing.

Damn.

Chapter Thirteen

Carlotta stared. Then blinked. Then stared again. And just for good measure, she blinked again, twice.

He was still there, standing like an avenging angel and appearing like a wild savage with his dark hair windblown and his clear eyes piercing through to her very soul. Even from across the room, she *felt* his presence. It overwhelmed her senses, blinding them to anything, anyone but him.

She could even smell him.

Why was he here? She knew he wouldn't have been pleased with her leaving, especially with what had transpired the night before, but... shouldn't he be grateful that she was now a woman of means? He didn't *have* to do the right thing anymore; she was able to care for herself.

Unless he didn't know that.

But she doubted that Lady Southridge would have kept that information from him. A more meddlesome, but kind, woman she'd never met.

And to think, Charles called her a soul of discretion.

Ha.

"Your grace?" she asked, her gaze fusing with his.

Melting into it.

Owning the truth she saw there.

Possession, pure and simple.

He came because, as far as he was concerned, she was *his*.

It was written all over his expression, in the hunger in his gaze, the power of his stance.

It easily could have made her angry, even offended that he thought she was in such desperate need of saving.

But it didn't.

Rather, it gave her the most overwhelming desire to hike up her skirts and run into his arms, knowing full well the moment she did, he be running towards her as well.

She stood then took a step forward only to be reminded of her guests' presence by the surprised welcome of Mr. Burrows.

"Your grace. What a surprise!" Mr. Burrows stood as well and walked over to the still quite savage looking duke.

"Mr. Burrows," he responded politely, but he never moved his gaze from her.

"Clairmont." Lord Darby stood as well, nodding his hello.

"Darby." The duke nodded again, still not removing his gaze from Carlotta.

"Would you please excuse us—" Carlotta began to speak, glancing to the other gentlemen it was easy to see the confusion and curiosity in their expressions.

"You left," the duke interrupted, taking a step forward. His voice captivated her attention and again, the room closed in till all that remained was her awareness of him.

"Yes." She could have said any number of excuses, but her will to fight left her. It seemed like that's exactly what she had been doing the entire time she'd known him. Run away. Thousands of reasons, good reasons, to avoid him, keep him at arm's length and reject even the slightest hope of having him. But with him chasing her to Garden Gate, not caring who saw the heat of his expression that was only for her, it melted her frozen resistance like the spring sun over snow.

And like that, her heart melted, as well as all of her excuses.

"Why... no. I can answer that question and the blame lies at my own feet." He shook his head slightly, his expression changing from the fierce passion of ownership of her very heart, to one of self-derision.

Carlotta ached for the pain apparent in his expression. Pain that she had caused in her efforts to protect her heart.

But what about his heart?

Who had been protecting it? For the first time she looked at the opposite side of things, much like Lady Southridge had explained last night. As if looking in a mirror, the entire view changed, righted itself and Carlotta realized just how much of a fool she had been.

But no longer.

When she had seen his reputation, he had been protecting hers by removing her from his gasp.

When she saw his title, he had lowered himself to love a servant.

When she questioned his honor in kissing her, he blamed himself for being so weak.

When she saw him compromising her to force her hand, he used the self-control of a saint, everything his very reputation testified against, and preserved her virtue even when she wasn't inclined to being virtuous.

"I never asked, I never said the right words. For one being known for saying all the *right* things, I'm pitifully miserable at speaking them to you. Carlotta, Lottie, *my* Lottie. I love you." Holding his hands out he waited, a man facing his uncertain destiny.

A destiny he had given her complete control over.

"I left this morning to get a special license for an occasion I failed to invite you to attend. You see..." He took another step forward, his gaze growing in determination, in resolve. "I seemed to forget to ask you a very important question last night." Another step forward, yet it felt like he was walking through the door to her heart, not knocking but simply walking through the door as if it never had existed in the first place.

And maybe it never had. Maybe... maybe he held the key all along and she never stopped resisting his love long enough to think of the possibility.

"Yes?" she felt herself ask. Her heart began to gallop within her, causing her body to tremble with a hope she never dreamed to unleash.

He glanced down and stepped around a settee, each step full of purpose... full of promise. "You have the impertinent habit of robbing me of all rational thought and I've never been as thoroughly overjoyed with a surprise as I was last night. I feel compelled to apologize for not asking you sooner, for being lost in the moment, as it were, and neglecting to speak my heart rather than simply acting on it. Carlotta, I'd ask you to marry me, but really, I'm quite accustomed to getting what I want. And if you refuse me, I'm warning you that I will likely create a scene. So rather, I'm asking you to take pity on me, and save me from my wretched self and marry me. Not because I deserve you, not because I'm a duke, or because I'm wealthy, but because I know that if you met me and I was penniless, you'd love me the same. Like you love me now, but won't admit."

"Create a scene?" she couldn't help but ask. A smile stretched across her face at the idea of the infamous, notoriously sinful Duke of Clairmont hanging propriety for the love of a governess. It was the stuff romantic dreams were made of.

Her romantic dreams.

That had somehow made it out of her dreams and into her real life.

"I'll simply have to compromise you. Believe me I have very credible witnesses." He gave a daring smile and mischievous nod to the gentlemen in the room.

"See here! There's no call to treat the lady in such a way!" Lord Darby's voice interrupted her sweet interlude, her secret satisfaction at the duke's willingness to create *that much* of a scene.

Never had she ever considered compromising so… romantic.

"Please, my lord." She held up her hand, sparing him only a slight glance before turning back to the duke. His eyes glowed with victory, a bright triumph shining from his expression. It was fierce and passionate, possessive and wild, full of love.

Love for her.

"Surely you can't stand by and allow—"

"Actually, Lord Darby, though his grace's reputation suggests otherwise, I have it on good authority that his intentions are quite noble, and have been for quite some time," Mr. Burrows commented.

"Carlotta?" the duke whispered her name.

Closing her eyes, she let the sound wash over her, owning the sound of his voice.

Tears pricked in her eyes as she considered just how close she had come to losing him.

"You're taking too damn long," he swore, his tone causing her eyes to flutter open only to find him striding towards her quite purposefully. A moment later he was crushing her to him, drinking in the passion of her kiss, demanding she surrender.

Which she willingly gave, with every last piece of her heart. Pressing into him she disregarded every warning she ever heard about acting like a lady and *owned* him with her kiss. As if tasting her answer, he deepened the exchange, his arms wrapping around her till every line of his was flush with hers, warming her, setting her on fire.

Gasping he broke the kiss. Hovering just a breath away from her lips. "Consider yourself properly compromised, Carlotta," he whispered.

"Indeed. Is your offer to make me an honest woman still stand? I seem to find myself in need of redemption," she murmured back, her cheeks flushed with her forward manner, but not repentant in the least for her actions, brazen as they were.

"No, the redeeming will be you're doing, not mine. I, however, will indeed save your surely blackened reputation. Even black knights sometimes ride white horses, my love."

Rather than answer, she lifted herself up on her tiptoes and placed a warm kiss to the edge of his jaw. "Then it is a very good thing you obtained a special license, your grace."

"You have no idea," he groaned and pulled her into a tight embrace, his nose burying in her hair, his warm breath tickling her scalp as he inhaled deeply.

"If I may be so bold?" Mr. Burrows interrupted.

The duke loosened his grip only slightly, turning he faced his solicitor, pulling Carlotta with him. It was as if he was afraid to let go.

She knew the feeling.

"Since I have all Miss Standhope's signatures, I'll simply await your notification after the wedding, your grace, to finalize a settlement on your new wife. I'll now take my leave. He bowed then turned to Lord Darby. "My Lord, thank you for your willingness to assist."

"Assist?" the duke asked.

"Yes… it would seem that you have quite a few friends who wish to secure your happiness. I'll let your wards explain the rest. Good-day."

Both gentlemen quit the room, leaving Carlotta quite alone with the duke.

Though she shouldn't be quite surprised.

She was a ruined woman after all.

"The girls?" she turned to the duke.

Charles narrowed his eyes slightly, as he stared at the wall. His expression was one of deep thought. "Were you... you weren't forcibly taken from Greenford Waters, were you?"

Carlotta shook her head, confusion fogging her mind.

"And you weren't planning on marrying Darby."

At this, she blushed and glanced away.

"Bloody hell."

"I wasn't going to marry him... I was simply offered the option." Shrugging her shoulders, she bit her lip.

"I think... that those three girls are possibly more meddlesome than Lady Southridge." He smirked, his expression humbled yet elated all at once.

"How so?"

"Oh, they put on quite the performance. Tears and all. Though I can't find it in my heart to be angry with them. After all, the outcome was quite perfect." He smiled down at her.

"Oh?"

"Yes. They gave me the excuse I needed to hunt you down and take you for my own prisoner."

"Had I no choice in the matter?" she teased.

"No, none. I believe I made sure of that."

"Indeed you did." She kissed his soft lips, savoring the rightness of his caress to the small of her back as he pressed her in closer, deepening the kiss by the intimate flick of his wicked tongue on the edge of her lower lip. Sighing her surrender, she pressed in further, committing the intoxicating flavor of his passion to memory as he groaned, his touch growing less gentle and far more demanding.

He groaned between his fierce kisses that were delightfully causing the glowing embers of desire to lick at her heels and threaten to consumer her. His hands roamed freely, as if he were a going blind and desperately trying to memorize each curve of her hip, the shape of her shoulders, the length of her neck, the weight of her —

She gasped as his hand caressed her breast, causing the burn of passion to immediately grow to an inferno. "Your grace..." she whispered, part plea for more and part plea for him to stop.

"Charles," he whispered against her lips, lowering his hand till it met the other in tracing her waist.

"Charles." She tasted the honey of his name on her lips, the intimacy of it was deeper than any kiss. It was a statement of her claim on his heart, the claim he had over hers.

"As I see it, there are two options available," he spoke silkily as he caressed her lips temptingly.

"Only two?" she teased, before leaning in for more of his kiss.

"Really I'd prefer to offer only one, but I find that being an engaged man has changed my morality for the better." He chuckled, breaking the kiss and gazing intently into her eyes. Mischief and desire waltzed with his expression, the perfect couple.

"That doesn't sound at all like you." Carlotta reached up and traced his jaw with her fingers.

"Damn you're making this difficult."

"What difficult."

"Being... good."

"Being good?"

"Yes, when all I want to do is show just how very wicked I can be. Because, love..." He leaned in, bending down he tugged on her frock till her creamy shoulder was exposed. As he exhaled over the skin, she immediately broke out in goose bumps from the heat then chill of his breath on her skin.

Then he kissed her, tasted her really. Lingering on her flesh as if savoring the flavor. Running the edge of his nose up the curve of her neck, he nipped, and teased the overly sensitive flesh with his tongue and teeth, causing Carlotta to forget what they were even talking about.

"As you can see, I can be quite wicked indeed. But this is not nearly, wicked enough for my taste. Which is exactly…" He paused at her jaw, moved his hands around till they cupped her bottom, swiftly pulling her in flush against him. "…why we need to leave. Because the only two options are leaving back to Greenford Waters so your girls can watch you get married, or for me to marry you here and I do *not* see a vicar in the room. Though to be fair, I haven't actually looked. I haven't wanted to look anywhere but at you."

Carlotta closed her eyes, letting his words, his touch wash over her. Like a warm and welcome spring rain, she soaked in the meaning, and realized anew how she was in sole possession of his heart.

And she had neglected to say something very important.

"I love you," she whispered the words, pledging them, vowing to protect his heart and guard it like the most sacred treasure.

Opening her eyes she glanced up, slightly shy. His blue eyes danced in victory, in joy. A fierce light illuminated his blue depths and almost stole her breath with the masculine beauty he possessed.

All because she had spoken the truth.

Perhaps, it did really set one free. Better yet, it set others free as well. As she lost herself in his gaze, she realized that he had been waiting for that very admission from her lips.

But not once did he push her, which went against his very nature.

"You no longer have two options. One, I'm leaving you one, and then *we're* leaving." His voice was thick with restraint.

"Oh? And what if I wish to stay?" She dared to admit the deepest desires of her heart.

"Then I will certainly fall under the temptation to take every inch of you, Lottie. But in doing so, I'll simply be acting as in my nature and you deserve far better than that. So, I beg of you, help me to keep my honorable intentions and let's be off. As it is, it will be dark when we arrive back home." He caressed her face lightly.

Home.

It was amazing how one word could open up so many emotions. Home was no longer Garden Gate, it was with him. *He* was her home.

"Then let us be off," she murmured.

"Thank God, and before you scold me, that was indeed a very reverent prayer."

Carlotta laughed.

"I find nothing humorous about this situation, madam!" But he grinned as he swept her up and all but ran out the door.

Chapter Fourteen

When they arrived at Greenford Waters, it was full dark and he was concerned that Lottie was perhaps catching a chill. He wrapped his arms around her tighter, pulling her soft body into his own, furthering his damnable need for her to extreme proportions. But his desire was secondary, first on his mind was her care. It was amazing how one person could become a man's whole world. His vision was tinted with the intense desire to protect her, care for her, *love* her. Every other emotion or need fell away in light of it.

And she had chosen him.

Rather, she had let him choose her.

And it was quite perfect.

"Are you too cold?" he asked, again. Honestly, he had lost track of how many times had asked that very question.

"Yes, I'm quite warm, your grace."

"Charles."

"Charles." She still spoke his name shyly, as if she couldn't quite believe she was saying it.

And every time she *did* say it, his heartbeat quickened and his body ached for her with a need he had never experienced.

Strangely enough, as delirious with desire as he had been this past evening, he had never found restraint easier.

Odd that.

At first, he had assumed it stemmed from the nature of his proposal. He'd never live it down once the word reached London.

But he couldn't care less.

As the shock wore off, he realized that his newfound powers of self-control stemmed from the fierce desire to protect her. Love had a way of changing the way a man saw things. When he thought about his past, he repressed the need to cringe. He wanted nothing of his past, his selfish and self-seeking nature to touch her, no. She was *not* one of the other countless women who had shared his bed for a night or two—she was different. She wouldn't be visiting his bed, but making it her bed too. He'd wake up with her every morning, have the delight of loving her, every delicious inch of her, each night. With the sun, she'd not disappear discretely, nor would she need her own apartment where he'd visit on his leisure. She'd bear their children, grow grey with him and nag him when they were both too old and deaf to hear each other.

The future had never looked so bright.

It was that very future that caused his restraint to be ironclad. Because this new life, new beginning was going to remain as perfect as he was able. Which demanded he wait.

And if anything spoke of the depth of his love, it was that he was determined to wait until they were married before he took her.

That wait alone might kill him.

But at least he'd die knowing he was honorable—for her.

Because in the end, it all came back to her.

After dismounting, he pulled her forward, kissing her deeply, searchingly till he could taste the honey of her desire filling his senses. Reluctantly, he released her and tugged on her hand while she stumbled dazedly toward the entrance.

Before they made it to the side entrance, the large wooden door swung open and the three girls rushed forward, running. If not for his intervention, they surely would have knocked his beloved Lottie to the ground.

Her smile was breathtaking, almost too beautiful to look at. Like staring at the sun, her face was lit up by the light flooding out from the wide open door.

All he could do was stare.

"Girls!" she shouted, her voice full of joy, relief.

They all hugged her at once, Berty, being Berty, was completely engulfed in her skirts while the two older girls hugged her waist. With tender caresses, she patted their heads, cupped their faces, and kissed their cheeks.

She would be a great mother.

Charles felt his grin grow wide.

A mother to *his* children.

Yes, it was a wonderful night.

"You're here! Oh, thank heavens! Charles how ever did you do it?" Lady Southridge exclaimed as she came out to meet them.

"It took some convincing," he replied, rocking back on his heels.

"Oh?"

Carlotta raised an eyebrow. "He was quite persuasive, Lady Southridge."

"Indeed I was." He met her warm gaze.

"And I have wonderful news. Tomorrow there will be a wedding." He spoke, not once taking his eyes from her.

"What? Hooray!" Berty jumped up and down, dancing. Then paused. "Wait… who's getting married?" She glanced at Lottie, then him, questioning.

"I am, Berty." Carlotta rushed forward and grasped the little girl's hands, spinning her around and pulling her into a tight hug.

"You are? To the duke? Oh, please tell me it's to the duke! We were trying so hard to—"

"Berty!" Bethanny's eyes widened.

"Yes, to the duke, Miss Berty." He chuckled. "And Bethanny, don't think we didn't see right through you." She had the good grace to look abashed.

"Oh, he didn't see through it till he had made quite a scene though, for that I thank you girls." Carlotta reached out and waited until the other girls joined her embrace.

"Quite a scene, Charles? It seems you have a story to tell."

"It's quite a story, Lady Southridge. As it is, I doubt he'll want to grace the door of White's for quite some time," Carlotta teased, giving him saucy grin.

His body coiled in tension, flaming to life and all it took was one smile. *Just one night.* He reminded himself. He only needed to practice restraint for one more night.

Perhaps he spoke to soon, rather thought too soon, about the whole restraint thing.

Maybe there was something to be said for impatience.

But as soon as the traitorous thought traveled across his imagination, he forced himself into check once more.

He would wait. He would.

But bloody hell if that smile of hers made it almost impossible.

"Well are we going to stand out here all night or can we go inside and hear the whole sordid tale?" Lady Southridge asked teasingly.

"Romantic, it was quite romantic," Carlotta corrected with a wink towards him.

Of course, when he was practicing herculean self-control, the temptress unveiled herself.

He should have known.

"Of course." Charles gestured towards the door. Knowing he had the longest night in his life stretching out endlessly before him.

****

He was right, the night went on forever.

And ever.

And then stretched longer still, until he was sure that God was holding off dawn just to spite him.

Though it would be quite merciful if he simply was holding off dawn when Charles knew he deserve far worse.

So he didn't complain, too much.

Finally, when the darkness was gaining the faintest touch of light, he rose and walked to the library. Immediately the memories from the past evening overtook him. The girls had admitted to a bit of planning… and stretching of the truth.

A lot of stretching, in his opinion.

They had been chided, without any heat to the scolding, and sent to bed after the tame version of the story. The version that didn't include his quite ruining kiss in front of his solicitor and fellow peer of the realm.

Although, he *was* surprised to discover the depth of the girls' involvement. It seemed that they had been conniving even before they left London, seeing the expression in his eyes, they said. He should quit playing cards at Whites, being in love made him easy to read, apparently. They further admitted to cornering Mr. Burrows and ironically, soliciting his aid. Mr. Burrows then explained that he'd have to speak with Lord Darby and well… the rest was history.

Quite humbling history, but history nonetheless.

Lady Southridge demanded the unedited version of their tale as soon as the girls left, and cackled in glee when she learned the desperate measures he had taken to insure Lottie's hand.

Her eyes rested on Lottie as she took her hand. "I'm so thankful he found you, so thankful."

Charles felt the need to clear his throat... just because he was in love didn't mean he necessarily wanted to wade in feminine emotions all evening. And if he didn't distract Lady Southridge, it would be a long and emotional evening indeed.

Thankfully, she took his hint and left them alone shortly after.

Alone.

For heaven's sake, the woman was mad.

Or maybe just desperate to make sure Carlotta was ruined enough to never make another escape.

Either way the temptation was enough to make him cross-eyed.

And he was far too pretty to be cross-eyed.

So he did the honorable thing, gave Carlotta a quick kiss, whispered, "I love you," and demanded that she lock her door.

And put a chair in front of it.

And if possible, her bed pushed against it as well.

Then he went to his own room, locked his own door, and stared at it. Trying very hard not to imagine what it would take to scale the outside wall and make it to her room alive.

But of course, the time he tried *not* to think of something, was the time that he could *only* think of that very thing,

In every possible way.

Which was why he was still awake after that eternal night, and was now pacing the library, trying very hard not to imagine what she looked like with her golden hair resting across her pillow, her eyes softly closed in sweet blissful slumber, or how seductive her expression would be when woken up with a morning kiss.

He groaned in agony. When did a vicar awaken? He glanced outside, noting the increasing light on the horizon. Maybe an hour more? He could survive an hour. One hour.

Sixty minutes.

But not one moment more.

****

Carlotta couldn't sleep. Every time she tried to close her eyes, his gaze would come into focus, stealing her breath and making her want to pinch herself. Just to make sure it was real.

All of it.

Biting her lip, she remembered his determined stride as he commanded her kiss, not caring for his own reputation but wanting her, needing her so badly that he was willing to do anything to have her.

He was brave enough for the both of them, because a part of her knew that if he showed even the slightest hesitation, it would have ended differently.

But it didn't,

It was rather like a fairy tale. The idea made her smile wider.

With a small sigh she rose from bed, it was full daylight now and she squealed in excitement knowing that today, this span of daylight would end with her being married...t o Charles.

Who also happened to be a duke.

A quite notorious duke.

Wonders never ceased. Ever.

A soft knock on the door interrupted her sweet musings. "Yes," she called.

Three girls rushed into her room, all speaking at once.

She grinned at her own foolishness at not taking the Duke's advice and locking her door. A reckless folly, to be sure, but one she was thrilled to indulge in.

"Do you know what you're going to wear? Bethanny asked, immediately going to her wardrobe.

"Can I do your hair?" Berty asked as she was hugged.

"You're getting married today!" Beatrix twirled, her face beaming.

"Yes, I am getting married today, girls! And I need your help! Bethanny? What do you think I should wear?"

An hour later, her dress was chosen, her hair braided, quite lopsided by Berty —she hadn't the heart to tell her she couldn't help, the braid was precarious enough that it would unwind on its own in a few moments, easily allowing her to seek the aid of a lady's maid for a proper coiffure— and Beatrix had smiled the entire morning, her face awash with excitement.

"I'm starving, can we please eat now?" Berty whined, even though she had a smile still lighting up her cherub-like countenance.

"Yes, I'm quite famished myself," Carlotta teased as she lightly touched Beatrix's nose.

"Carlotta?" Lady Southridge's voice called through the closed door to her chamber.

"Yes?" Carlotta opened the door.

"You're a vision... except, well..." Her eyes took in the lopsided braid. But before she could comment, Carlotta glanced meaningfully to Berty, who was beaming. "Your hair is lovely." She nodded.

Quick woman, that Lady Southridge.

"We have much to do if you're getting married today. To think! No waiting for the banns, no church! Charles should be ashamed of himself." It would have sounded like a scolding, had she not been smiling the whole time she said it, or clapping her hands excitedly. "You'll be gossip of the year... of course I'll make sure everyone knows it was a love match, an impatient one. Not one out of necessity." She nodded sternly.

"Er, yes," Carlotta agreed, her face heating. Of course, that would be easily proven false in year when she didn't give birth to the duke's heir after an exceptionally short term.

But it still was nice, knowing she had a force like Lady Southridge in her corner.

Because the woman was, indeed, a force.

"We'll breakfast and then hopefully Charles will have returned. It seems he's already left... strange man. You'd think he'd want to be with his future bride." She clicked her tongue and led them all away towards the dining hall, the girls following behind, giggling and asking a million questions about the special day.

The question of the duke's whereabouts was answered as they were finishing breakfast, when he arrived with a very disgruntled vicar in tow.

"Are you ready?"

"You can't be serious!" Lady Southridge stood as she tossed her napkin on the table.

"My question was not aimed at you, madam." The duke spared her only a glance.

"But it's... simply not done! She needs to have her hair properly... er..." Lady Southridge glanced to Berty. "It's needs to be re-braided," she finished, which was the truth as it was slowly coming unwound.

"Oh! I can fix that!" Berty took the words as her cue and rushed around the table to re-braid the ends of her hair.

"Perfect! Now, are you ready?" the duke asked again, walking over towards Carlotta and placing a quick kiss on her lips.

"For?" she asked, quite perfectly pleased at his show of affection. She could get used to morning kisses at the breakfast table... dinner kisses, bedtime kisses. *Especially bedtime kisses.*

"To get married?"

"I don't believe I've ever seen a more eager groom. Quite odd," Lady Southridge commented, her fingers resting on her chin as if deep in thought.

"Eager, dedicated, stubborn, take your pick, but I'm starting to wonder if I'm talking to myself since I'm not getting any answers," the duke grumbled.

And, because really there was nothing else to say. "Yes,"

Carlotta answered. While she would have wished for a few more moments to ready herself, as she dwelled on it, this was quite perfect.

And appropriate.

Her hair was braided, lovingly —if not lopsided— by Berty.

The duke, *Charles*, she reminded herself, was simply being himself. Demanding... all because he loved her that much.

Lady Southridge was meddling, because, that was simply what she *did*.

And Bethanny and Beatrix had excused themselves quite silently and were now returning with some flowers they had pilfered from the gardens. The little minxes!

What more could she ask for?

"Delightful! I was beginning to think I needed to cause another scene... but a man can only do so many before he gets a complex."

"I have all faith your ego will survive." Lady Southridge shook her head.

He glared at her.

"Shall we?" Carlotta stood and walked towards the vicar who had been watching the exchange with avid interest and found it amusing enough to grin slightly.

At least she thought it was a grin.

It might have been annoyance but she chose to believe it was a grin. This was her day, after all.

"My lady," the duke offered her his arm, and escorted her to the small prayer chapel within Greenford Waters. It was a cozy room, with wooden hewn crosses and stained glass windows that let in amber colored light. Flowers dotted the altars, and candles flickered in the colored light.

"It's beautiful," Carlotta whispered as they walked in.

"I'm thankful you appreciate my efforts," the duke commented.

"*You* did this?" She glanced over at him, her eyes wide.

"Of course! It's not as if I have no forethought," he grumbled, then grinned. "Of course, Tibbs helped."

"The plot thickens."

He raised an eyebrow then paused. "I, well. Should I walk you in then? Or would you rather… it seems I didn't have as much forethought as I believed. Dash it all. You're walking in with me." He answered his own question. "Berty? Bethanny? Beatrix, follow Miss Lottie. Lady Southridge? Get Tibbs, I want another witness."

Lady Southridge nodded and left, returning less than a minute later with a very satisfied looking Butler.

"Now." The duke glanced around, and finding that all was in order. Turning to Carlotta, he asked. "Shall we?"

He asked, he did not demand, nor push her down the aisle —which she didn't think he'd hesitate to do, rather endearing, that. Rather, he *asked*.

"I love you." She reached up and caressed his face with her gloved hand, her fingers trailing the line of his jaw.

"This damn wedding cannot happen soon enough," he cursed, then pulled her in. His hands wound around her back, pulling her flush against his body while his mouth met hers in a hungry passion.

The vicar cleared his throat.

Berty gagged.

And Lady Southridge chuckled. "My, my how the mighty have fallen."

"You try my patience, Miss Lottie. Are you ready?" he whispered against her lips, the sweet scent of peppermint and desire intoxicating her.

"Yes."

"Finally," he replied and led her down the short aisle.

Chapter Fifteen

The wedding was long. So long that Berty and Beatrix fell asleep on Lady Southridge, who wasn't in much better shape if her constant head bobbing was any indication. In hindsight, Charles thought that perhaps it was the vicar's only way at retribution for being woken up at the break of dawn.

Apparently, *this* vicar wasn't an early riser.

Therefore, after not one, but *two* sermons on the virtue of patience and brotherly love —which he didn't see the relevance for at a wedding, for heaven's sake, *brotherly* love?— and an especially long vow process —including vows he had never heard of at any other wedding, ever —since when did a man promise his wife a pig?— Charles was finally convinced the end was in sight.

He should have known better.

After yet another sermon —this one on self-control, which was causing him to quickly loose whatever control he'd *had*— the vicar pronounced them man and wife —and Charles silently swore that the vicar would be finding a new parish to preside over.

It was only eleven in the morning when all was said and

done, and Charles was not in any mood to wait till nightfall. So, after being quite patient through a luncheon prepared by the Greenford Water's staff, he made their excuses and, to the amused grin of Lady Southridge, stole his wife away. Far away. Thankfully he had heard Lady Southridge mention a picnic to the girls.

He knew he loved that woman.

Or at least liked her. He could afford to be charitable since it *was* his wedding day.

And so, without any hesitation, he swept his beautiful wife into his arms, and strode purposefully down the hall.

"I can walk," Carlotta murmured against his neck, as she buried her head there in a decidedly contented fashion.

"No, not fast enough."

"Impatient?"

"You have no idea, and I actually think I have been quite patient! Any other woman would have been proposing to me at my first blink in their direction! You, I had to chase across half of England."

"How trying for you."

"Indeed. But lucky for you, I find you worth the effort."

Carlotta laughed, a deeply seductive sound that made him increase his pace, and not a moment too soon, they entered his room. He set her down, kissed her quickly and then turned and locked the door. And for good measure, he put a chair in front too.

Nothing was going to interrupt him.

Nothing was going to interrupt *this*.

****

Slowly, with measured grace he circled her, his eyes roaming every inch, setting her on fire with his gaze alone. Wherever his gaze landed felt like a fiery touch, igniting a passion within her that she didn't know existed.

And she suspected it was only the beginning.

Mercy.

His eyes, so light and mischievous usually, smoldered with blue fire. With one deliberate step after another, he slowly strode towards her, his gaze never leaving hers, freezing her in place as she waited, breathless for whatever happened next.

Because honestly, she hadn't much of a clue as to what happened next. She knew it was intimate, she knew a few basic particulars, but beyond that? Nothing. Yet she didn't feel fear or even embarrassment at her lack of knowledge, rather an anticipation for her very thorough education.

Because the duke, *Charles,* was nothing if not thorough.

She inhaled deeply, letting the moment overcome all other senses. Closing her eyes, she waited. A moment before his lips caressed hers ever so gently, she felt his warmth against her skin, heating her without even a touch. Tenderly, he traced the seam of her lips till she opened them, welcoming his caressing tongue as he began the dance, one she could only follow as he led.

Pressing for more, she leaned into him, demanding more of his kiss, but he didn't give in to her demands, he backed away.

"No love, the anticipation, it is part of the glory, and possibly the most important part," he whispered against her lips then nibbled them wickedly.

"Anticipation?"

"Yes…" he murmured then bowed to kiss the curve of her jaw.

Her eyes closed in passion and all she could hear was the sound of her heart, the sound of his breathing.

His very measured breathing against the gasps of her own.

"Why aren't you as affected?" she lowered her chin to meet his gaze, insecurity slithering into her heart like black ink.

"Not affected?" His eyes widened and he took a step back. "Every inch of me is demanding I take you without even the slightest or smallest precursor to lovemaking. Your name is a litany in my mind, whispered by my heart every time it beats. The fact that I'm wanting to make this the most amazing..." He kissed her neck once more. "...blissful, reverent, and erotic experience you'll ever have... until the next time... and the time after that till I'm too old to see straight." He chuckled against her skin, inhaling deeply. "I want to remember every moment, every scent that I inhale off your fragrant and flushed skin. I'm far more affected than I might seem because if I even allow the slightest lapse in my self-control, this will be over before I even have a chance to begin.

"I've made my share of mistakes, Carlotta. This will not, be one of them. I'm not simply making love to you, I'm giving you everything I am." He murmured against her skin, his hands caressing her shoulders and pausing at the ribbons of her dress, unlacing it. A moment later, it pooled at her feet in a heap of lavender silk. The warmth from his hands saturated her soul, melting her into a world where nothing apart from him existed. Kissing her neck his hands wound around her back, deftly undoing each button until none remained. Her skin was feverish, overly warm yet she trembled, never having been so exposed to another person.

And she was still in her underpinnings.

Softly, he tugged, unlaced, and removed every last barrier. His touch was methodical, possessive and like sparks causing her body to ignite in a delicious fever. Once finished, he reached down lacing his fingers within hers, gripping them tightly as he slowly let his gaze travel down, stepping back he took her in, completely bare.

The embarrassment that she anticipated in such an intimacy never surfaced. Rather she found that she felt bolder.

Stronger. Like she had faced her greatest fear and realized it was never a fear to begin with. Taking a deep breath, she smiled and lifted their interlaced hands... and spun slowly, like a dance. His gasp caused her to smile, a knowing smile that only a woman as desired, as loved as she could ever experience. With their hands still raised, he released her hand and trailed his caress down her arms, flowing over her most sensitive areas and resting on her stomach. He pressed into her belly till she stepped back and she was flush against him. Her eyes drifted closed.

"I love you," he whispered as he kissed her neck. "But I do believe I'm reaching my limits..."

"Oh?"

"Hmm," he murmured against her skin as his hands roamed her hips, squeezing them and rubbing his jaw against the curve of her shoulder.

"Perhaps I can help." Turning in his arms, she reached up, glanced up into his smoldering gaze and began to untie his cravat. The soft silk floated to the floor. Reaching up on her toes, she kissed his neck as she began to unbutton his white shirt after she removed his jacket. His pulse raced against her lips, his breathing far more unsteady than earlier.

Carlotta rejoiced in the knowledge that she was the one causing it.

Once his shirt was loosened she slid her hands over his warm chest, across the hardened planes until it fell to the floor along with his cravat and coat. With a wicked grin, one she didn't know she possessed, she reached down to remove the last barriers between them. Biting her lip, she made quick work of the remaining clothing till she was free to do some exploring of her own.

Taking a step back, she followed his example earlier and walked in a slow circle, studying him, memorizing every hardened plane and every valley in the 'V' of his back. Never could she have imagined the magnificent appearance of a naked man. He was perfect, solid, strong and gazing at her as if there was no one else in the world. She stilled, not quite knowing what to do next.

She should have known that he'd take command.

He always did.

Without a word he swept her into his arms and laid her on the bed, covering her with his body as he kissed her deeply, his hands raking over her body in desperation

An emotion she was learning to appreciate.

He was so warm, setting her skin on fire every place his skin touched hers.

Which was everywhere.

It was delicious, it was overwhelming. It was perfect.

"I—Carlotta, I might... as in... the first time I might cause you some pain."

"Pain?"

"Bloody hell... please tell me you know what I'm talking about," he swore, his face a mask of determined passion.

"I trust you," she whispered, closing her eyes and giving herself over to the feel of him.

"But—"

"I trust you, Charles. I love you, I'm quite mad with it, if you cannot already tell. There's nothing I want more than for you to make me yours. In. Every. Way."

"Carlotta." He groaned and kissed her fiercely, as if a man starved.

Then he moved.

And everything Carlotta imagined about the intimacy of marriage was put to shame as she discovered what the physical act of love could do.

Her world rose.

It fell.

It shattered into a million pieces of light.

And never had she felt more whole. More loved.

It was the amazing feeling of being completed and

realizing the missing piece she had always been missing was found in someone else. Not herself.

It was blissful, amazing and she had the whole experience to look forward to for the rest of her life.

Charles pulled her into the cocoon of his warmth as he lay beside her. His soft breath tickled her hair as she leaned against him and felt the rapid beating of his heart against her back, knowing hers was pounding just as hard.

"I love you," she murmured against his arm as it curved around her, pulling her in tight.

"I love you." He took in a breath, as if preparing to say something then thinking better of it.

"What were you going to say?" she asked, turning in his embrace to face him.

"I was going to say something then thought better of it."

"Oh? Why?"

"Because I want nothing more than to live, to dwell in this perfect moment. Life happens, Carlotta, but when these perfect moments happen, you have to live in them, own them, commit them to memory so that you have them with you always."

"When did you get so wise?"

"I have had the unfortunate necessity of learning from my mistakes."

"Haven't we all?"

"Perhaps, but I have quite a list of sins, my love." He paused and raised an eyebrow. "What I was going to say was... never in all my life, my sordid, blasted and black past have I ever experienced what we completed this night, ever. Nor could I have ever imagined that love could feel like this. What I'm trying to say is that whatever my sins, that is one thing I can give you that I've given no one else. You have my heart. It's never been given to another and in that, you are my first, my last and only."

"Thank you," she whispered and kissed his forehead,

closing her eyes and doing just as he suggested; owning the moment, memorizing it. "I'll guard it with my life. Guard mine too."

"With my life."

****

Good Lord, why weren't there more children in the world?

So maybe it wasn't the most romantic thought, it was still the first thought in Carlotta's mind when she awoke, nestled in the shelter of her husband's arms, with his very warm, very tempting skin on hers, and her memory all to vivid from their night of passion.

Yes, it was a strange thing that there were not thousands of babies born every day if *that* was how it came about.

Groggily he shifted so that the sheet covering her didn't actually cover her any longer. For a split second, she thought about pulling it up.

For propriety sake.

And then realized she was being quite proper being undressed, naked, and languid.

Because she was married. Every warning flag of passion was now a white flag of surrender. It was intoxicating, it was freeing and it gave her imagination far too much to work with.

Sighing in satisfaction, she nestled deeper into his embrace, drinking in the scent, the sunlight spinning into their room, the soft cadence of his breathing.

And was home.

****

Charles awoke to the soft press of his wife's body nestled into his chest. Before he even opened his eyes, he could smell the sweet scent of her skin, the fragrance of her hair... *lemons?* And the perfect curve of her hips fitting against his.

And gone was the tranquil moment.

Rather, all he wanted to do was explore her again, and again and then after perhaps a break for food and water... again. Every experience he had prior to last night was pathetic, cheap and a rather poor imitation of what love could really fell like.

It was poetic; deeper than the physical, it was stronger than any words, it was... without description. But he felt it all the same. Deep in his heart, his soul.

It was madness.

It was absolutely perfect and he couldn't wait for each new sunrise where he'd find himself beside his *wife*.

With a wicked grin, he allowed his gaze to greedily take in her exposed shoulder, creamy and soft, perfectly curved, a delightful preamble to the curves to be found just beyond.

He placed a kiss to the very sensitive place he discovered last night, right where her neck and shoulder meet, and lingered there, teasing the flesh with his tongue.

"You're awake." She spoke softly, a grin evident in her tone.

"Indeed," he murmured against her skin.

If she were planning on saying anything else, he'd never know. Because before she had a chance, he was spinning her around, finding the sweet delight of her mouth and restarting everything they explored the night before.

Epilogue

"You're beautiful! Miss Lottie!" Berty spun around her chambers, her dress sailing out like an umbrella. They had debated on what the girls should call her now, technically she wasn't a 'miss' any longer, but old habits die hard, and well... it was quite nostalgic to hear their voices call her 'Miss Lottie' still. Though Charles had requested they used 'your grace' in front of company.

Which wasn't often.

Thank goodness. It had been several weeks and she still couldn't quite believe she was a duchess.

Duchess.

No matter how many times she repeated it, it never stuck. But she suspected it was because she didn't actually care for the title, rather she simply cared for the man who gave it to her.

Charles.

"Are you ready yet, Love? There's a fine line between fashionably late and simply late," Charles teased as he made his way into the room. But before he could finish the teasing remark, he paused.

"Take it off."

"What?" Carlotta blushed crimson and glanced to Berty, who had paused mid twirl with a very confused look on her face.

"You cannot wear that!" Charles' gaze darkened, much like it did when alone with her… and she was well… *taking it off.*

"Charles!"

"Not—" He glanced to Berty quickly. "—like *that.*" He shook his head as if her coming to that conclusion was insane. "You… It… I'm a jealous man, Carlotta, and if one dandy so much as blinks in the direction of your… charms…" He coughed with a quick glance to Berty, who was watching with rapt attention. "Well, I'll not be responsible for my actions," he finished.

"But… this is what Lady Southridge picked for me to wear to our first ball."

"Bloody hell, I should have guessed. That damn woman will kill me."

"I think she looks like a fairy princess," Berty added, helpfully.

"Berty." Charles paused then walked gently to the little girl. Bending down he met her at eye level. "Carlotta is the most beautiful, most perfect princess in the world. Never once did I mean that she was not. Forgive my outburst, young lady. If you are so set on the dress, then she may wear it. Provided… she doesn't leave my side and she wears a very large fur cape."

"Large fur cape?" Carlotta asked with a daring raise of her eyebrow.

"Very, very large."

"But then no one will see her dress!"

"Exactly."

"You never use to be so stuffy," she crossed her arms, narrowing her childlike gaze at him.

"I—" He closed his mouth. Narrowed his eyes and... then grinned.

"I suppose finding out I have a heart after all does that to a man," he teased, tickling her nose with his finger.

Carlotta held her smile in check, she was so thankful for the deepening of the relationship between the girls and her husband. Being married had brought out a protective side she would have never assumed existed.

But exist it did, quite fiercely.

Heaven help the suitors who pursued the girls.

"Your grace." Berty rolled her eyes, but grinned. "So she can wear the dress?"

"Yes. But I injure a man. I'm blaming you.

"Very well." She shrugged and walked away, leaving them alone.

"So yes or no?" Carlotta pointed the dress, spinning slowly."

"Only if I get the honor of taking it off... and possibly mangling it so that you cannot wear it again," he teased as he strode forward and kissed her favorite spot just at the base of her neck.

"We'll be late."

"I don't care."

"Yes you do."

"No. I do not. Quit arguing with me."

"I—"

"Miss Lottie!" Bethanny strode in, her face flushed and her eyes dancing.

"Yes?" Carlotta backed away from his embrace, cheeks flushing as well, but quite curious as to Bethanny's expression.

"You have guest. Actually *two* guests, but Lady Southridge isn't exactly a guest, she's family."

"Oh? Who is the other guest?" Carlotta asked before Charles could make a remark.

Bethanny blushed deeper, her eyes lowering for a

moment. "Lord Graham, her brother. I've been informed that he's just returned from Scotland." She finished, but her tone was far more breathless at the end of her statement then at the beginning.

What if...

"We'll see him immediately," Carlotta nodded, her curiosity flaring.

"We will? Yes..."Charles cleared his throat." We will." He gave Carlotta a confused expression and then furrowed his brow as his gaze dipped lower, and then rose again a question in his eyes.

"Later," she whispered, then followed Bethanny out.

Not for the first time, Carlotta took note of how Bethanny was growing up, growing into herself. Her long chestnut hair was heavy and curled just enough to make it a dream to work with. Her figure had filled out as well, and like a mother watching her baby chick try to fly, Carlotta felt her throat constrict at the idea that someday, possibly soon, she'd test her wings.

They arrived in the red parlor in their London home. The same parlor that had been filled, utterly filled with well wishers, and the insanely curious, *ton* upon their arrival not so long ago. The ball tonight was to introduce the Duchess Clairmont to the world.

Lord Graham was facing the window; looking very much like the first time she had met him. His sandy blond hair and green eyes were every bit as dangerous as Charles, but there was a teasing light to him, a lack of brooding that gave him a far less intimidating manner. His face lit up in a warming grin when he turned around upon their entrance.

"You devil! I didn't think you'd actually take my advice!" Lord Graham teased, striding forward and shaking Charles' hand.

"And you, Duchess Clairmont. A pleasure." He bowed and lifted her hand to his lips, his eyes dancing with a teasing light.

Charles growled.

"Possessive, are we?"

"Yes. Very. Now back off, Graham. I'm in no mood."

"I can see that... and here I thought marriage would have turned you into a pussy cat... or at least a lap dog."

"Ha!" Carlotta laughed, covering her mouth with her glove too late.

Lord Graham cast an amused grin her way.

Carlotta took that moment to find Bethanny. Sure enough, she hadn't left, but was watching Lord Graham with rapt attention, her eyes soft.

"Have you met Bethanny, my lord?" Carlotta asked.

"Yes, I believe I have, but not formally. Miss Bethanny, I'm pleased to make your acquaintance."

Bethanny's face blushed vermillion, her smile was beatific, her eyes took on a flirtations glint Carlotta didn't know she could do, and of course, at that moment Lady Southridge walked in.

But the two being introduced didn't notice her.

Carlotta did... and saw the smile... the raised eyebrow and the overjoyed nod that accompanied her quick assessment of the situation.

Good Lord, here we go again.

More by Kristin Vayden

To Refuse A Rake

Emma has sworn off love.

After all, it is pointless to subject oneself to such torture when in the end, heartbreak is inevitable. Just like her sister had suffered. So, when Lord Daventry, the muddy brown-eyed boy from her childhood, returns to society she refuses to even look at him... well, maybe she'll look once.

Or twice.

But only because his eyes have changed into the most decadent color of dark chocolate. And his tanned skin from his travels is distracting, especially paired with his wide and devilish grin.

The stirring of her blood from his hot whisper in her ear is nothing... at least that's what she tells herself.

Lord Daventry has one response to marriage. Drink Brandy. Especially when his mother decides it is time for him to produce an heir. Reluctantly, he attends his first ball since returning from India, swearing to head to White's shortly after the first dance. However, he is pleasantly surprised to discover that Miss Emma Kingsly, the same girl he tried to kiss when she was nine, is still unmarried.

Her frigid demeanor should have warned him off... but unable to ignore a challenge, he plunges in head first... never expecting to fall in love with the one woman in the ton completely set against marriage.

Redeeming the Deception of Grace

Lady Grace Hashiver has perfected the art of hiding behind a sarcastic wit when it comes to dealing with the rakish Ewan Emmett Duke of Greys, her childhood tormentor. It's her only weapon, for if she let her guard down even for a moment; surely he'd know just how much she loved him. A love she knew could never happen.

Ewan Emmett, Duke of Greys is perfectly thrilled to torment Grace at every opportunity, until an old acquaintance begins an honest suit for Grace's hand. When Ewan begins to feel the pangs of jealousy causing him to question his reasons for his constant teasing of Grace, he discovers a depth of emotion he didn't know he harbored towards the golden haired beauty. Suddenly he is not longer the tease, but on the receiving end of the torment as he wonders if he's too late to fight for her love.

Sometimes, all love needs is a little healthy competition. Wouldn't you agree?

Knight of the Highlander

Colin is not who he claims to be…

His position as the blacksmith of Clan Chattan is simply a cover, a means to an end. He was sent with one mission; find Jacobite loyalists and eliminate their threat. But that's not what keeps him up at night, or what burns hotter than his forge. The most dangerous threat is one of his own making; falling in love.

Arywnn knows someone is watching her…

In her dreams he's handsome, braw, and willing to take her away from her reclusive mother and tyrant laird father. But her daydreams are a frivolity she cannot afford, not while a spy lurks within their clan. Worse yet, her father has promised her hand to whomever discovers the blackguard.

A midnight meeting…

A whispered kiss…

And a rogue English knight all change the course of destiny in a way neither could have ever imagined.

Colin must play a dangerous game, but the prize is worth

the risk; Arywnn's heart.

Living London
Book One of the Westin Legacy

Love is stronger than we can imagine.

Love is never impossible. But for Joselyn Westin, it's not probable. After the death of her grandmother, Joselyn feels lost in world that seems empty, till a cryptic message in one of her grandmother's favorite books changes everything.

Sometimes love happens in the most unexpected, incredible places. Jocelyn wakes up in London, during the Regency Era. But her knowledge of the time is poorly lacking, even with all the historical romances she's read. She quickly learns that life is the greatest teacher.

What Joselyn discovers is more than just history, it's a way of living, a way of loving and discovering that for love, nothing is impossible.

Especially when you find yourself "Living London."

Surviving Scotland
Book Two of the Westin Legacy

Only love is strong enough to grasp what it was never meant to have.

Elle can't deny that Ioan is handsome. That is, until he opens his mouth. How can someone so masculine and striking be so irritating? Yet part of her knows that if his sarcastic and teasing temper changed, she'd lose her heart.

Ioan knows that Elle is untouchable. To protect his heart, he keeps her at arm's length with incessant teasing and a quick wit. She can never know the truth. But like a moth drawn to the flame he can't resist her. Indeed he already burned.

When the Jacobites attack Carnasserie castle, the Black Watch come to assist. Though Elle has her own personal battle to win, they both with learn that Surviving Scotland isn't for the faint of heart...

Beyond Broken

He was searching for hope in a world that offered him everything. With his life spiraling out of control, he sought salvation at a rehab center, never expecting to find light after admitting all the darkness he carried. The last thing he needed, was to fall in love.

But sometimes we can't choose who we love--it chooses us. And that what she did; she chose him, mind, body, and soul. And he was helpless in love's grasp.

She knew his name spelled trouble, but was unable to distance her heart until it was too late, until it already deep within his grasp. Sometimes, even when you want to help those you love, even when you have the best intentions--they have to love themselves enough to want to change.

Nobody ever said love was easy, and for them? The battle has just begun.

Beyond Broken is a NA romance with a very strong inspirational thread. However, it is still not considered a religious or inspirational romance because of the elemental theme of drug abuse, sex, and strong language

Pursued

When everything falls apart, you're faced with two choices. Do you lose your faith or do you really begin to live it?

For Abby, she chooses to walk by faith, and in turn God takes the smoldering ashes of her world and begins to bring her to life.

Levi Jensen was waiting for the right woman. He'd made

his share of mistakes and refused to settle for just anyone. But he never thought God would bring him a petite blonde with two children. But Levi soon learns that God's plans are always better than our own.

God created romance. Abby and Levi learn first hand, that through difficulties, hardship and mistakes, God brings about beauty for ashes. He always writes the best love stories. The kind that last forever.

Made in the USA
Columbia, SC
23 November 2019